THE SPIDER:
THE WHEEL OF DEATH

MASTER OF MEN!

THE SPIDER®

THE WHEEL OF DEATH

By R.T.M. Scott

ALTUS PRESS • 2019

CHAPTER 1
THE VERMILION SEAL

DUSK WAS falling and the lights were turned on in Grogan's Restaurant. It was a small, gloomy place, with a dozen round tables and two curtained booths where special customers could eat and talk unseen. At the rear were two still smaller rooms, the kitchen and beside it a tiny cubicle of an office which contained Grogan's battered desk and an old-fashioned iron safe.

It was rumored that things happened in Grogan's Restaurant, things which were best kept hidden from the honest light of day. It was said that narcotics could be bought there, and it was whispered that young girls had entered the place and never again been seen by their friends. The West Side police of Manhattan had visited the place many times. But Grogan made no objection to such visits, and the police found nothing. Yet the rumors and the whispers persisted.

Burly Dan Grogan stood now near the rickety cash register, his yellowed teeth clamped tenaciously about an unlighted cigar. He had only three customers. Two men, hard-eyed and low-voiced, were smoking and drinking in one of the booths. At the back of the restaurant, near the door of the room which contained Grogan's safe and desk, was a man with plastered hair and high-waisted trousers who was consuming his third cup of coffee.

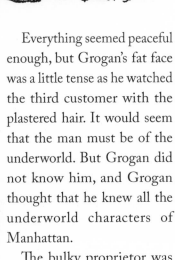

Everything seemed peaceful enough, but Grogan's fat face was a little tense as he watched the third customer with the plastered hair. It would seem that the man must be of the underworld. But Grogan did not know him, and Grogan thought that he knew all the underworld characters of Manhattan.

The bulky proprietor was curious and uneasy. Things often happened in his small restaurant when he became uneasy. And when things did happen they usually happened so fast that he liked to be prepared. The stranger might be an imported gunman, waiting

2

to rub out one of his best customers in some criminal feud. Dan strolled over to the stranger.

"You from Chi?" he asked, complementing the man by naming the second largest city in America.

"What's it to you?" snapped the stranger, looking up at the proprietor with cold, shrewd eyes.

"Not a thing, my friend." Grogan was accustomed to hard characters and he knew how to handle them, sometimes politely and sometimes brutally. He was being polite to this man who had made him curious and strangely uneasy. "Got a name?" he asked, smiling.

"Any name," was the curt answer. "Try Dick."

Grogan shrugged, rumbled a laugh and moved back to the cash register, to stand chewing his cigar while his eyes wandered continually back to the man who had called himself Dick. The stranger impressed him as a man who might prove useful.

MEANWHILE, DICK lit a cigarette and, without seeming to do so, strained his ears in the direction of the booth where the other two customers sat drinking and smoking. By listening intently, he was able to catch a few words of their conversation. Perhaps, as they drank more, they might speak more loudly. Dick waited patiently and called for another cup of coffee.

Then the door of the restaurant opened and a girl came in. She was young and slim and pretty. Her face was delicate and indicated that she was not accustomed to such a restaurant, nor to the characters who frequented it.

As she took a seat at a table, Grogan looked at her in frank surprise and one of the men in the booth pulled the curtain aside to peer curiously out at her.

The booth curtains fell hurriedly into place, and the voices behind them became so low that they could not be heard at all. The solitary waiter brought a fourth cup of coffee to the lone stranger. But the man called Dick left it untouched. He sat without motion, a cigarette drooping between his lips, apparently engrossed in deep thought.

The curtains of the booth parted again, and one of the two

men came out. He was a little drunk, and he smiled ingratiatingly as he approached the girl at the table.

"Will you join us for a real drink behind the curtains, kid?" he asked, bending over her so that his breath must have been in her face.

The girl looked nervously at the dirty table cloth, as she tried to ignore him. She was not the kind who could handle drunken men in Grogan's Restaurant. The "silly" hat, probably purchased for a dollar and her one effort to be smart, was pathetic upon the side of her head as she looked down, crimsoning.

"Come on, kid," the man insisted, seating himself beside her and rubbing a hand over her shoulder. Then, as an afterthought, he asked hastily: "Waiting for somebody?"

"Waiting for me."

It was the stranger at the far table who had spoken. Perfectly motionless, in face and body, he sent the three words past the cigarette between his lips.

"Is that so?" The slightly drunken man was in a nasty mood. He rose from beside the girl and faced the stranger "And who the hell are you?"

"None of your damned business!" retorted Dick coldly. "Get back in your stall, if you want to keep a whole skin."

The man swayed a little, but reached with a significant motion toward his hip pocket. The stranger sprang to his feet with his hand under his coat. It was a tense moment. In another second death would stalk—not for the first time—in that tawdry little restaurant of evil rumors and whisperings.

"Cut it out, Joe!" The words came in a roar from Dan Grogan, whose big bulk lumbered with surprising speed to a position between the two men. "You're drunk, Joe! Get back to your table."

Joe obeyed sullenly after a moment of hesitation. Dick remained standing with his hand still under his coat.

"And you, stranger, sit down!"

"Go to hell!"

Big Dan Grogan stared at the stranger, shrugged his huge shoulders and broke into a smile. "Drink your coffee standing up if you like it that way," he grinned with seeming good nature. But on returning once more to the cash register, his hand touched a revolver which lay beneath a sheet of paper on a little table beside him. It was well to be prepared. The atmosphere of the restaurant was charged with the possibility of sudden destruction.

INSTEAD OF sitting down at his own table the stranger deliberately strolled across to the girl's and sat down beside her. His action was easy and natural and there was no smile or leer upon his face. He had seated himself so that he faced the curtains of the booth, but his back was to Grogan.

"Name's Dick," he said. "What's yours?"

He said it so naturally that, after one glance into his eyes, she answered quite as simply: "Molly."

It was one of those rare, self introductions which are instantaneously genuine. He, flashily costumed, and she, in her cheap but becoming little dress and saucy hat, had become friends during the passage of a few seconds. Probably it was her helplessness and his eyes which worked the friendship. The best in man comes to the surface in response to a woman in need of help; and some men have eyes which women instinctively trust.

"What are you doing here?" he asked in a voice so low that only she could hear.

"It's Grogan," she returned in an equally low voice.

"You know something about him?"

She nodded.

And there their conversation ended. Behind his back Dick heard the deep voice of Dan Grogan.

"I want to talk to you privately," Grogan was saying. "Come back to my office and have a drink."

The man who called himself Dick rose from his chair, touched the girl's hand, reassuringly, as he left the table and with face expressionless followed the proprietor silently into the little back room which contained the battered desk and the iron safe. In continued silence he took a chair and stared up at the pictures of boxers which hung upon the walls while Grogan, seated before his desk, filled two small glasses with whisky from a long-necked bottle.

"Here's how!" exclaimed Grogan, raising his glass.

"I don't drink," resumed Dick, leaving his glass untouched.

Grogan grunted and gulped his own drink without further hesitation. "Never hold that against any man," he commented, wiping his mouth, "Lots of good men killed every year by drink."

There was a silence. "What's your line?"

"Nearly any line." Grogan raised his eyebrows. "Dope?"

"Maybe."

"Women?"

Dick did not reply.

"Well," said Grogan, "women are dirty business, but there's money in them."

The proprietor's guest yawned rather insultingly and seemed to be interested in inspecting his slightly pinkened finger nails.

"Look here, Dick, as you call yourself," continued Grogan, "you got guts and you're a quick thinker. I'm interested in you. Can't we get together?"

"Maybe."

Grogan considered. "I've got to know what you can really do."

"I've handled dope—in big lots, nothing small."

Grogan frowned. "I'd have to have some proof of that—names, you know, that I could look up. Got anything on you that I could check on?"

Dick, his face always expressionless, shook his head. "Never carry anything that anybody could check on," he said. "Wait a minute. I might be able to show you something."

He drew a silk handkerchief from his sleeve, brushed his finger tips gently with it for a moment and knelt beside the old-fashioned iron safe. With an ear against the iron door he gently, very gently, touched the dial with his finger tips and began slowly to turn it while Grogan bent forward, intensely interested.

IN THE incredibly short time of about two minutes the kneeling man seized the handle and pulled open the heavy door.

Grogan lurched swiftly out of his chair and slammed the

door closed again. But his fat face was wreathed in smiles. "You've got what it takes, Mister!" he exclaimed. "And how!"

Dick calmly rubbed the dial with his silk handkerchief to remove his finger prints and resumed his chair. "A child could open that box," he remarked contemptuously.

"And can you use soup too?" asked Grogan with much enthusiasm.

"Yeah! But there aren't many boxes I have to blow."

Grogan was so pleased with the man he had found that he poured himself another drink and was in the act of gulping it, when a feminine scream sounded from the restaurant.

Through the door, into the little square room, came Joe, carrying Molly in his arms. He was holding her roughly and had a hand over her mouth to prevent another scream. Behind him came his companion, looking both angry and alarmed.

In language shockingly blasphemous Grogan demanded an explanation as Joe flung the girl into a chair where she huddled, too scared to move or cry out.

Joe's explanation was that the girl had been eavesdropping, listening to their conversation behind the curtains of the booth. He had seen her ankles below the curtain and had peeked over the top of the partition and caught her.

Dick shot a single swift glance at Molly when he heard she had been listening to the two men he himself had been trying to overhear. Then he turned indifferently away and looked at the boxing pictures on the wall as if the affair were none of his business.

"Well, what did she hear?" asked Grogan savagely. But he

didn't wait for an answer. "It doesn't matter," he snapped. "She's asked for it, and we can't afford to take chances. I'll get my car. We'll soon put her where she'll do no more snooping."

"I don't care," interrupted Molly in a pitiful voice. "You are killing my father, Dan Grogan! You—you might as well kill me too." But she was after all only a very young girl. Her head fell sidewise as she spoke and she fainted.

Suddenly Grogan turned to Dick. "Stranger, you seem to have butted into something."

"Butted nothing!" retorted Dick sharply, wheeling about from his inspection of the pictures on the wall. "You asked me to come in here."

"Yeah, but now that you're here, you'll stay—till I know you better. Joe, hold him till I get back with the car. And don't forget that he's as sharp as a cop's whistle."

With these words Dan Grogan lumbered out of the back room, and the slamming of the front door indicated that he had left the little eating place.

DICK FOUND himself looking into the muzzle of Joe's revolver from almost half way across the small room, too far for him to reach it swiftly enough with a hand. Out of the corner of his eye he could see the inert form of little Molly, half slipping out of the chair.

Slowly, almost magically, the stranger's bearing began to change, the cheapness of the underworld seeming to fade from him.

"Joe," he said highly, "I'm afraid I cannot comply with Mr. Grogan's request to remain."

"The hell, you can't!" exclaimed Joe savagely. "Try anythin', an' you'll get a bullet through your head."

Joe never spoke again. With the deftness of a French boxer, Dick shot his right foot upward. His toe caught Joe's wrist, and the menacing revolver clattered upon the floor. Simultaneously two blue-black pistols seemed to leap into the strange man's hands from beneath his coat. The two guns roared together, with one sound but with two targets. Joe and his companion were dead before they struck the floor!

Very calmly, without the least trace of concern, the strange man dropped his weapons into their holsters beneath his coat. Then he swung open the safe door which Grogan had neglected to relock. For a few seconds he crammed papers into his pockets, but he did not take some packages of opium, recognizable by their smell. He closed the safe and turned toward the nearest dead man as if he were about to perform some act.

Then, from the restaurant, outside, a heavy step sounded. The man named Dick drew back from the dead man and crept swiftly to the door which was almost closed. He peered through a narrow crack. A policeman had entered the restaurant, no doubt having heard the shots, and was hesitating by the cash register while he looked around.

The peering man crept back into the little room. He had very little time in which to act. Rapidly he took out his cigarette lighter and, from a secret compartment in it, extracted a tiny seal which he pressed upon the foreheads of the dead men in quick succession.

And where he pressed that seal there remained the vermilion

outline of a spider. The Spider, the unknown killer of New York, had made another killing.

This audacious act performed, almost in the face of the law, the self-possessed man emerged from the back room, wildly gesticulating toward the kitchen door for the benefit of the policeman who had not been quite sure that the sound which had attracted him had really been a pistol shot.

Ahead of the policeman Dick opened the kitchen door and stuck his head into that room for a moment while he pointed alarmingly toward the open back window for the benefit of the cook and waiter who were already badly frightened.

What followed, followed quickly. The cook and waiter, desperately frightened, struggled through the window, one after the other, in an attempt to escape from whatever danger might be approaching. The policeman charged into the kitchen and continued through the window, thinking that he was pursuing escaping criminals.

Dick darted again into the little back room. He picked up the unconscious Molly as easily as if she had been a kitten and carried her through the empty restaurant into the street, where a girl in a man's arms is soon forgotten by New Yorkers when a taxi spirits the two of them into a New York night....

CHAPTER 2
PURSUIT

S TRANGE THINGS happen in New York taxis, especially after dark. There are horrid things and disgusting
things which occur in the semi-seclusion of these cabs as they
whirl through the lighted streets of the city. Young girls have
their lives wrecked, and old men are made foolish by the clinging playthings of Broadway. There are robberies, murders and
even more ugly crimes committed behind the backs of the
drivers. A passer-by catches but a glimpse, and the driver is
often too bored to look into the little mirror which reveals what
is going on behind him when the blinds are not drawn to cut
off his view.

As the taxi sped away from Grogan's Restaurant with the
man and the unconscious girl, the driver suspected that something was wrong. But he had seized the crumpled bank note
which had been thrust into his hand and he had opened it
sufficiently to see that it was a fifty-dollar bill. And he had
heard the magic words: "There's another one coming."

In his little apartment uptown he had a wife and five kids
to feed. Also he knew that a driver sometimes received a bullet
in the back when he did not do what he was told to do. So he
drove on, turning into the stream of traffic flowing north upon
an avenue.

And behind the driver's back the man who called himself
Dick supported the girl with his left arm while, with his right
hand, he extracted another fifty-dollar bill from a well-filled

13

pocketbook. Through a glazed window of the pocketbook was exposed a New York Police Department pistol permit. The name on the permit was Richard Wentworth, and the address was one of the most fashionable sections of Park Avenue.

It was evident that the man with the plastered hair had not lied when he had intimated that his name was Dick. But not one of his fashionable friends would have believed it possible for the fashionable Richard Wentworth to carry away a young lady in a fainting condition, from so tawdry an eating place as Grogan's Restaurant. His friends would not even have recognized him if they had passed him on the street in his present disguise.

But few of his friends really knew much about Richard Wentworth. Occasionally he flashed into public view upon the polo field. At times he was reported to be engaged in adventurous enterprises in far-away countries. At other times his name was connected with police investigations of criminal activities. In his clubs and in the drawing-rooms of New York he was seldom seen. It was usually where danger and excitement dwelt that Richard Wentworth might be found.

It was this liking for danger which had brought him, that night, to Grogan's restaurant whose sinister secret, if uncovered in time, would, he believed mean the saving of many lives and much misery.

As the taxi rolled northward, Wentworth lit a cigarette with his free hand and watched Molly as she began to recover consciousness. He was, he knew, in a difficult situation. No man can tell how a strange woman will come out of a faint. Some women snap back to full life very quickly; others are slow and sometimes very sick. Molly might be hysterical and attract police attention by screaming. And police attention was the last thing that Wentworth desired. The Spider would undoubtedly be sent to the electric chair, if he were ever apprehended. And the Spider's death seal was upon the foreheads of the two men in Grogan's Restaurant. Certainly the two men had deserved the death penalty, but the law does not permit private individuals to become agents of justice—even when the law fails, itself, to bring deserved punishment.

Molly moved her head, with its short, fair curls, upon Wentworth's shoulder. Her blue eyes fluttered open and closed again. She really had very pretty hair, Wentworth observed, and her skin was clear and almost without make-up. Dressed fashionably, she might have been beautiful. Yet the driver, who was shooting glances into his little mirror, wondered why a man would spend as much as fifty dollars for such a girl when he might easily have one quite wide awake for a fraction of that amount.

"Turn into Central Park," directed Wentworth as they came to 59th Street, "and keep going."

The spoken words roused Molly to complete consciousness. She lifted her head from Wentworth's shoulder and stared wildly around her. It was a tense moment. If she became hysterical or lost control of herself through fright, Wentworth might have a very difficult situation to face. It would be almost impossible for him to explain his position to a policeman. But awkward problems and difficult situations, especially if accom-

panied by danger, were the wine of life to Richard Wentworth. He waited. A few moments would tell the story.

"Hey, mister!" It was the driver speaking as they swung into Central Park. "Do you know that we are being followed? There's a blue, closed car just behind us. I've been watching it for the last half mile."

WENTWORTH GLANCED back and saw the car. There

16

It would be in passing, while the two cars were traveling at almost the
same speed, that the machine-gun bullets would sweep the taxi.

were two men in the tonneau beside the driver. Certainly it was
not a police car, which meant that it must belong to some
member of the underworld. Wentworth had another problem
upon his hands, a problem that might be far more dangerous
than the problem of Molly.

"Keep on going," he ordered the taxi driver quietly. "I'll tell you what to do in a few minutes."

The driver did as he was told, but he was nervous. He suspected that they were being followed by some members of the criminal world which infested the great city in which he worked. And he knew that disagreements among criminals often ended in a hail of bullets. He edged out to the left and shot his car ahead of the slower traffic. But the blue car followed closely.

Meanwhile Molly did the unexpected thing by leaning back in her corner of the cab and commencing to cry and sob as if her heart would break. She had looked at Wentworth and recognized him as the man who had sat, uninvited, at her table. But she showed no fear. Her sobbing was obviously the expression of heartbreaking grief—not of terror.

Wentworth knew women. He let Molly cry briefly while he glanced back and saw that the blue car was still following them. He saw something more. One of the men in the tonneau seemed to be lifting a bulky object from the floor and adjusting it. He could not be certain, but the man seemed to be handling a machine gun. In the shadows of the tonneau the other man appeared to be very large and to resemble Grogan.

The situation was becoming complicated. Central Park offers many stretches of road where, at night, traffic is slight and where a burst of machine-gun fire can be delivered with impunity by bold criminals.

Wentworth turned to the girl. "There is nothing to be afraid of, Molly," he said.

"I'm not afraid," she replied, sobbing. "I just don't care any more. It—it's too late to care now!"

Wentworth considered this reply, but could not understand it. However, there was the blue car to think about. He felt that he had to think about that car, if he and Molly were to go on living. He had been watching the following car guardedly through the rear window of the taxi and once, under a road lamp, he had recognized big Dan Grogan beyond any chance of mistake.

Grogan could have no reason for the pursuit except to bring death to the two occupants of the taxi.

THE TAXI driver also had been studying the pursuing car by means of his rear-view mirror, and he was becoming more and more nervous. He knew his New York, and he thought that his wife and kids needed him more than he needed the second fifty.

"I don't like it, mister," he said, beginning to slow his taxi. "You'll have to get out and walk."

Wentworth said nothing, but he partly exposed a pistol from under his coat. Molly did not see the weapon. The driver, however, saw it in his little mirror, and the taxi shot ahead again.

"You are a good girl not to be afraid, Molly," Wentworth said, speaking pleasantly and easily. "But why is it too late to care now?"

"You wouldn't care much about anything if your father was going to die tonight, would you?" she asked.

Wentworth caught his breath in surprise. He had been very

fond of his father, who had been killed in the war—in the same battle in which he, himself, had been seriously wounded.

"What made you ask that question?" he inquired, looking at her gravely.

"Because my father is going to be electrocuted at ten o'clock tonight."

Wentworth flipped his wrist over and glanced at the watch which was strapped upon it. It was half past eight. He looked down at the little girl beside him and saw that her eyes were flooded with tears.

Behind them Grogan's blue car was creeping up and was turning out to pass them. It would be in passing, while the two cars were traveling at almost the same speed, that the stream of machine gun bullets would sweep into the taxi.

"Jam on your brakes!" barked Wentworth at the driver.

"Hard, man! If you want to live!"

The brakes of the taxi screamed as the car came to such a sudden stop that Wentworth had to hold Molly to prevent her from being hurled forward off the seat. At the same time the blue car shot past them too fast for any marksman to take aim and fire. As the other car disappeared around a bend in the road, the taxi driver looked back at Wentworth and positively refused to go on. Since it was a one-way road there was nothing to do except stay where they were at the side of the road. To go back against the traffic would mean running foul of a traffic policeman. And policemen were almost as dangerous to Wentworth as were the criminals who were after his scalp.

"All right," he said quietly to the driver. "Smoke a cigarette and get back your nerve."

"It isn't a case of nerve, Mister," the driver argued. "It's a case of common sense. I saw what they had in that blue car, and I'm not paid to get my head blown off."

As the taxi stood by the roadside Wentworth turned again to Molly. "What is your father's name?" he asked.

"Arnold Dennis."

Then Wentworth understood. Arnold Dennis had been a bookkeeper for the Mack Syndicate, a wealthy corporation which handled a great deal of contract work for the city, chiefly the supplying of materials for construction work. Dennis had been convicted of the murder of a junior partner of the company while working overtime very late at night.

At the trial evidence was given that the junior partner had caught Dennis falsifying the books and had been shot by the elderly bookkeeper in an endeavor to cover up his crime. The pistol had been exhibited, bearing Dennis' finger prints.

MOLLY DENNIS had at last stopped crying. But there was hopeless misery upon her young face. Her father had an hour and a half to live, and the tragedy of it was more than she could bear.

"But what were you doing in Grogan's Restaurant, Molly?" asked Wentworth.

"Father was framed," she answered. "He described the real murderer to me, but he didn't know his name. He also told me that the Mack Syndicate had some dealings with Dan Grogan, entered in a secret ledger which Mortimer Mack, President of the Mack Syndicate, kept in his private safe at home."

Wentworth looked at her sharply. If this were true, he had not been far wrong in his assumptions concerning Grogan's restaurant. He was on the trail of one of the greatest scandals in the history of New York! For if the Mack Syndicate, famed for its large business deals with the city, had any kind of commerce with a man like Dan Grogan, it could only mean one thing—that the seeming respectability of the syndicate cloaked shocking corruption of the most sinister sort.

Yet Wentworth, for the moment at least, was more interested in the human story of Molly and her father than he was in the possibility of some great crime in the making.

"But what were you doing in Grogan's Restaurant, Molly?" he persisted.

She told him that she had been looking for the real murderer; and that Grogan closely resembled the description given her by her father. That night, in desperation, she had risked an open visit to the restaurant, praying that she might gather some new evidence to free her father. And she had overheard sufficient of the conversation in the curtained booth to make it evident that Grogan was known in the underworld as the real murderer of the junior partner of the Mack Syndicate!

There was no doubt regarding Molly's truthfulness. Wentworth had only to look at her to know that she was sincere. It was possible, even probable, that her father was innocent. Nothing was too hideous to be possible if such a firm as the Mack Syndicate had undercover dealings with Dan Grogan.

Such a condition of corruption was the kind of thing which, above all else, Richard Wentworth loved to fight. And, when the happiness of a young girl was also at stake, he asked for nothing better.

But he wondered grimly whether in this case the odds against him were not too great to overcome. A man must die in less than one hour and a half. Could he stop the execution? He was in a taxi in Central Park. His clothes were such that his friends would be shocked if they saw him. Only the Governor of the State of New York could reprieve the man who was to be executed so soon. Governors are difficult people to reach quickly, and they are not easy to influence. In the case of Arnold Dennis, condemned to death, Wentworth had no new evidence which would be accepted in a court of law.

But he had faith in himself, and he loved a fight.

"Molly—"he began. Then broke off abruptly, as the taxi driver gave a shout of alarm.

Backing down the road toward them came the blue car which had passed them. Something barrel-like and menacing projected from the rear window of the backing car.

The taxi driver flung wide his door and leaped into the park, racing across the open space. For Wentworth to have followed him, even if he had been unencumbered by Molly, would have been suicidal. He would have been shot down before he had covered twenty-five yards of the open space.

"Molly," Wentworth said, taking her hand and touching her for the first time since she had recovered consciousness, "let's make a fight of it."

And in the second before Richard Wentworth went into action her eyes glistened. He smiled. There was satisfaction in fighting for an Irish girl with courage....

CHAPTER 3
WENTWORTH TELEPHONES—
UNDER DIFFICULTIES!

THE BLUE car, backing toward the stationary taxi, had arrived within about thirty paces and was slowing to a stop preparatory, no doubt, to spurting away after riddling the taxi with bullets. From its rear window could plainly be seen the barrel of what must be a machine gun. But there was no light in the tonneau and the men behind the gun were invisible.

It would have been possible for Wentworth to shoot into the blue car as it approached. But he could not see the men in that car, and a burst of machine gun bullets would probably have wiped him out before he had found his target. It was necessary for him to do something else—and to do it instantly!

The escaping taxi driver had left his door open and his engine running. Wentworth took advantage of both conditions. He had scarcely dropped Molly's hand before he had opened his own door, stepped upon the running board and had slipped into the driver's seat.

Richard Wentworth could drive any make of car more easily than most men can work a gum-slot machine. He released the brakes, threw in the clutch and gave the engine all the gas that is possible in starting. The heavy taxi lurched into motion violently. It gathered speed in a way that is only possible when an expert handles the controls. Even so, no taxi can run away from a machine gun.

But running away was not in Wentworth's mind. To attempt to flee would be what any murderers would expect him to do under the circumstances. And much of Wentworth's success was attributable to the fact that he seldom did what he was expected to do.

The heavy taxi rushed forward, gathering speed. It did not swerve to the right or left, but headed straight for the murder car which had now stopped!

A collision was inevitable. Machine gun bullets might possibly kill the driver of the taxi. But no bullets could stop the rushing taxi before the rear end collision took place. A machine gunner is unnerved by such a condition. He is like a sniper who tries to pick off the pilot of a tank while lying in the direct course of oncoming destruction.

He may get the pilot, but the tank will get him.

Wentworth, calculating on the psychological effect upon the machine gunner, took the only course which permitted him to attack. And his ruse was successful in that the crash came before the machine gun opened fire.

Although the collision was severe it was not too severe for the bumpers to withstand. The heavy taxi bunted the lighter car violently forward. The barrel of the machine gun was tilted upward by the heavy jar, and a burst of bullets, fired probably by accident, traveled high toward Columbus Square.

Wentworth sprang out of the taxi and thrust a hand under his coat for a pistol, as he ran forward to come to grips with his enemy before they could recover from the demoralization of the collision. "Once on the run, keep 'em on the run," was Wentworth's idea of good tactics in any fight.

But Wentworth had two surprises. The blue car leaped forward and vanished around a bend in the park road and—his hand found an empty holster under his coat!

The escape of his enemy was probably a good thing for him under the circumstances, but the empty holster caused him to frown. The pistol which it had held was registered with the New York Police Department in his name. Had he dropped it in Grogan's Restaurant while bending down beside the iron safe? He could not be sure, but the loss of the pistol might prove serious. If it came into the hands of the police, it might conceivably send him to the electric chair.

WENTWORTH PATTED his other holster, which was still filled and returned to the taxi.

Molly Dennis was waiting for him. She was not crying, and seemed to be calmer. No outcry had come from her at the time of the collision with the murder car.

"You are not afraid of me?" asked Wentworth, more to judge her condition by the tone of her voice than for any answer she might give.

She shook her head. "I'm not afraid of anything in the world except for my father." Her voice was firm, though it broke a trifle on the last few words.

He slipped into the driver's seat. "I'll do the best I can for you," he said and looked back at her through the open window behind him. "Remember, Molly, if you work with me, you must know that there is no such thing as defeat. Now I'll show you how a taxi should *not* be driven in New York City."

He slipped in the clutch and the taxi moved swiftly along the shadowy road of the great park. Once more he was launched upon a grim battle against the powers of the underworld, with a man's life the stakes of victory or defeat. To win he must play a desperate game. In that game he held a certain ace which he hated to play. But, for Molly's sake, he would play it if it became necessary to do so.

Rapidly the taxi swept northward and turned out of the park at the first exit to Fifth Avenue. Not once did Wentworth see any sign of the blue car with the murderous machine gun, and he believed that Dan Grogan had probably abandoned the chase. He felt certain, however, that he and Grogan had not ended their fight. There was no doubt that it would be renewed and that death would come to one of them. But Grogan, dangerous as he was, was only an underling. In the battle that was to follow there would be enemies far more important and powerful than Grogan for Wentworth to encounter.

As they turned into Fifth Avenue and joined the southbound traffic, Molly reached forward and touched Wentworth back through the open window.

"The blue car!" she called to him. "It's right behind us."

Wentworth glanced back. It was quite true. She had seen what he had not seen. He could not see into the car, but he recognized it without any doubt and he knew that Grogan had not been shaken off for the evening. It might be that Grogan intended to attack him again, even on Fifth Avenue. And it might be that Grogan was following him only to discover his identity.

Wentworth shot the cab ahead of car after car in the traffic, dodging in and out with the greatest skill and audacity. Behind him the blue car followed with equal skill. He caught a traffic light just as it turned to red, but the blue car followed him against the light and the traffic officer failed to blow his whistle.

At the next corner Wentworth drew up at the curb and lifted his hood, pretending to examine his engine. The blue car shot by and stopped at the curb a hundred yards farther on, ready to turn and go back if Wentworth tried to escape by turning abruptly northward.

Wentworth looked at his watch. It was nine o'clock. In one hour Molly's father would die, burned to death in the electric chair at Sing Sing. Dangerous as it was for him to allow Dan Grogan, or any other man for that matter, to discover his real identity, Wentworth decided that there was no time for him to shake off his pursuer if he was to fight for the happiness of the girl behind him in the taxi. It was necessary, he realized, for him to sacrifice his own interests and his own safety for another.

Wentworth slammed the hood into place over the engine and climbed back into the driver's seat. As he had stopped at a corner, he turned east and raced across town. But at Lexington Avenue, where he turned south again, the blue car was only half a block behind him.

AFTER SOME fast driving, several times almost drawing

the attention of a traffic officer, he stopped before a cheap apartment house close to the East River and hurried with Molly into the narrow entrance just as the blue car drew up behind the taxi.

It was a "walk up" building, and Wentworth almost lifted Molly as he rushed her up the stairs. Footsteps sounded behind them on the first stairs as they turned into the second flight. But Wentworth felt that he dare not stop to fight while he had the girl in his care. Besides, it was vitally necessary for him to reach the Governor of New York State immediately, if Molly's father were to see another dawn.

On the second landing Wentworth opened a door with a key which he had ready in his hand and shoved Molly ahead of him into a small two-room apartment. As he entered himself and closed the door, he heard heavy footsteps of their pursuers in the hall outside.

Before them in the living room of the small apartment, a tan Hindu rose from the floor where he had been squatting before the elephant headed god of luck, Ganesh. Ram Singh was devoted to Richard Wentworth and believed that his master was omnipotent in all things. But Ram Singh also believed in propitiating the gods and, when his master used strange disguises and mixed with the wicked people of the world, Ram Singh burned incense before old Ganesh. In this way the Hindu servant believed that his master would gain the god's protection and become invulnerable amid the dangers which might surround him.

Molly had started in surprise, a little alarmed at sight of the

Hindu, but Ram Singh showed no surprise at all upon beholding the slip of a girl accompanying his master. Although many of his countrymen believed that a woman had no soul, he had been taught by his master that all women must be respected. In addition, for all he knew, this little girl might be a princess in disguise. Was not his master dressed in the clothes of a loafer and bad man of the street?

"This is Ram Singh, Molly," Wentworth said upon entering. And to Ram Singh: "Dennis, *missie sahib,* Ram Singh."

As the Hindu lifted his hands to his forehead in silent salutations, Wentworth picked up the telephone, perhaps the only private telephone in that cheap apartment building, and asked to be connected with the Governor's personal secretary at Albany.

Molly Dennis seated herself upon a chair in the sparsely furnished room. She was tense and nervous. So much depended upon the telephone call which this strange man was making. Her father's life hung in the balance. Her eyes wandered restlessly from the man at the telephone to the incense burning in the little saucer before the strange image of something with an elephant's head and four arms. It seemed impossible that such a man, living in such a place, could have any influence with so important a man as the Governor of New York.

But Molly did not know that Wentworth maintained the meager little apartment under a fictitious name for the sole purpose of assuming his disguises when he secretly penetrated the underworld of New York City. She did not know that a large closet in the bedroom was crammed with clothing, some of which would fit almost any character which Wentworth might wish to assume. Nor did she know that Ram Singh was a master of make-up and that he could alter a man's face astonishingly in a very few minutes.

MINUTES PASSED and Wentworth kept his eyes on his watch. But he held it so that Molly did not know that he was watching it. There was only half an hour left. The chaplain was probably with the doomed man in the death cell.

Then Wentworth was talking with the Governor's secretary. The call had gone through. But of course the secretary could do nothing. Wentworth merely gave his name and asked to be connected with the Governor as quickly as possible. The secretary replied that the Governor was attending an important conference and could not be disturbed for some little time.

"I know him well," Wentworth insisted. "Tell him that it is a matter of life and death and that I must speak to him at once."

He was afraid to say more. Governors are guarded against importuners just before an execution.

Molly sat rigidly upon her chair, her face becoming tense with apprehension. She had been buoyed up more than she had realized, and now she began to feel that she had been clinging to a straw.

Wentworth glanced at her and back to his watch. He, too, was under a strain, but he did not show it except that an old battle scar was showing white under the skin of his forehead. Usually quite invisible, it sometimes showed white at moments of great stress.

The secretary was speaking again. The Governor, he said,

would come to the telephone in two or three minutes. Wentworth thanked the secretary and looked again at his watch.

"How much more time is there?" asked Molly tremulously. This time she had noticed the direction of Wentworth's eyes.

"Plenty of time," he answered calmly, but he did not look at her. "We will win. Don't fear!"

There was a knock upon the door of the apartment. Ram Singh came out of the bedroom and moved across the living room toward the front door, but stopped at a word from his master.

Wentworth began speaking Hindustani to his servant, while he continued to hold the receiver of the telephone to his ear. The tall native threw back his shoulders, and an indignant rage showed in his glittering, black eyes. He spoke gutturally in reply to what he had heard. If a bad man wished to disturb his master while he was telephoning, he, Ram Singh, would go out into the hall and cut that bad man into small pieces.

But Wentworth shook his head and spoke more words of direction in the servant's language.

Ram Singh drew a long knife from the sleeve of his coat and squatted upon the floor facing the door, the knife in his hand. It was a beautiful knife with a heavy, carved handle. The blade was sharp and pointed. It could be used equally well for both cutting and stabbing, and it was perfectly balanced for throwing.

In the room there was brief silence, broken presently by a crashing sound at the door. Someone had thrown his shoulder against the panel. Perhaps several men were trying to force it.

The door was not strong, and could not, Wentworth knew, resist a great deal of force.

WENTWORTH, PERFECTLY calm, continued to hold the receiver of the telephone to his ear. With his free hand he drew his remaining pistol from its holster and held it lightly on his knee. He sat so still that he seemed scarcely to be breathing, but his blue-gray, calculating eyes wandered from Molly to Ram Singh and from Ram Singh to the watch on his wrist.

There came another crash against the door.

"Go in the bedroom, Molly!" Wentworth suddenly ordered.

"No!" she refused emphatically. "I'll stay and fight with you."

"Do you want me to hang up this telephone?" he asked quietly, his eyes on the door.

Even as she fled through the door, terror stricken at the possibility of his breaking the telephone connection, he was talking again, this time over the telephone. The Governor was on the other end of the wire and Wentworth was speaking in short, sharp sentences to conserve time as his eyes watched the creeping hand of his watch.

The Governor was obdurate. He could not reprieve Arnold Dennis, even for a week, without legal evidence of the convicted man's innocence.

Again came a terrific shock on the apartment door, which was plainly upon the point of giving way. Ram Singh rose from the floor and stood in a crouching position, knife in hand.

Molly came to the bedroom door and stood with her knees shaking while she listened to the words of the man at the telephone.

"Governor," Wentworth said, pistol raised and watching the door for the next shock upon it, "for my own sake I would never say what I am going to say; but I once saved your daughter's life when she fell off your yacht at Oyster Bay. I am fighting for the happiness of the daughter of Arnold Dennis. In return for what I did at Oyster Bay, I want you to give me one week in which to prove that Arnold Dennis is innocent."

Wentworth spoke only one more word over the telephone.

"Thanks," he said as he replaced the receiver.

Molly Dennis flung herself across the room at Wentworth's feet. But he picked her up, carried her to the bedroom and playfully tossed her halfway across the room onto the bed.

Then he turned back to the living room. "Open the door, Ram Singh," he said, "and let our friends come in."

CHAPTER 4
BEHIND THE BARRICADE

WENTWORTH'S IDEA in ordering the opening of the door was twofold. He wished to do the unexpected thing, and he wanted to finish the present affair so that he could get away from the apartment. He had been traced to this hideout place of his, and its usefulness to him was ended. Somewhere in the vastness of New York it would be necessary for him to establish another place where he might lose his identity and from which he could emerge in the various disguises he used.

His present problem was to make his departure as soon as

possible, without disclosing his real identity either to the underworld or to the police.

As he stood to one side of the room, with his pistol held lightly against his hip, there was a trace of boyish carelessness about him. He seemed to have gained a lightness of heart from the moment that he had hung up the telephone. The reprieve of Arnold Dennis had been his first objective and he had reached it. A week lay before him in which to prove to the Governor that his request had been just, and much may be done in a week by a man like Richard Wentworth.

The pistol, held with such apparent carelessness, covered the door which Ram Singh stealthily approached. It was a deadly weapon, capable of ejecting the empty shells and substituting new cartridges in the barrel as fast as the trigger could be pulled. And Wentworth could handle it, as he could any kind of a firearm, with a fatal accuracy which was little less than wizardry.

Ram Singh silently drew back the bolt and placed his hand upon the door knob. In his other hand he held the big knife.

Wentworth turned his body slightly so that the muzzle of his pistol could not be seen by anybody standing in the doorway when the door was opened. Yet he could fire instantly, if necessary, by advancing the hand which rested against his hip.

Then Ram Singh swung the door swiftly open and stood unseen behind it.

Standing in the doorway was a man with a revolver in his hand. That man was in uniform, and upon his breast was the shield of the New York police!

Wentworth could have shot the man before him. He could have shot him in the heart, in the head or through the shield upon his breast. But Wentworth did not shoot policemen. He fought policemen, when he was forced to fight them, only with the cleverness of his mind.

Standing perfectly still, he faced the uniformed man without the slightest indication of surprise. He wondered if his lost pistol had already been identified by the police and if, in some way, they had traced him to this apartment.

Instead of advancing his pistol hand, resting against his hip, he drew it gently backward and, unseen, slipped the pistol into his hip pocket. Then he dropped the hand to his side…. Desperate as the situation might prove to be, he must depend upon his wits and not upon the force of bullets.

"Come out of there, fella!" commanded the officer, keeping Wentworth covered with the revolver.

Wentworth frowned. "There must be some mistake, officer, I—"

"Mistake, nothing! Come out of there!"

Wentworth took a few paces forward as if he were about to comply with the order. Out of the corner of his eye he saw Ram Singh standing rigidly and unseen behind the door he had opened, waiting for an order from his master or for some indication of what should be done.

"What is the charge?" asked Wentworth, halting half way across the room and hoping to gain some bit of information.

"You'll hear the charge at the station house," answered the policeman. "Shake a leg, mister!"

It was then that Wentworth discovered something. He saw that which even his sharp eyes had failed to note up to that moment. *The policeman was wearing patent leather shoes.*

No New York policeman would wear patent leather shoes in uniform while on duty. Therefore the man before him was no policeman at all.

Too late Wentworth realized that he was facing one of Grogan's criminals. The man had him covered, and any attempt to reach back into his hip pocket for his own weapon would almost certainly mean instant death!

IN THE few seconds before he spoke again, Wentworth tried to figure out why the masquerader had not shot him at once upon entering. If only he knew the reason for this delay, he might still be able to extricate himself by means of his wits. Two explanations seemed possible. His enemies might be afraid of the sound of a shot, fearing the intervention of the police. Or the other, more plausible one that they did not know who he was and wished to find out something about him before they killed him. Wentworth decided to probe the possibility of this second explanation.

"You must have the wrong bird, officer," he said. "Who do you think I am?"

The man hesitated, and Wentworth felt that he was on the right track. "You don't even know my name," he complained. "You sure have the wrong bird, officer."

"Well, what is your name?" demanded the pseudo-policeman, lowering his gun a trifle.

Suddenly a way to escape flashed into Wentworth's mind.

The man's question had given him a chance to speak to Ram Singh without the knowledge of his enemy! "My name," said Wentworth, "is *Darwaza Bundo.*"

Crash! The door was slammed and bolted by the quick thinking Ram Singh almost as the words *"darwaza bundo"* were uttered—those words, in Hindustani, meaning "shut the door."

In the hall there were angry exclamations. Footsteps sounded as men crowded around the door without any attempt at concealment. There was loud and irritated conversation. The apartment house was the kind which housed people who sometimes fought and who sometimes became noisy with drink. It required very serious disorders to attract much attention in that building.

After a few moments of thought Wentworth came to a decision. He desired to leave that apartment secretly and without leaving behind him any trace of himself or of his activities. He also desired to take Molly away so that nobody would know she had ever been there.

The door trembled again under the weight of several shoulders from without. That weakening door was the first thing which had to be attended to and, from the bedroom, Wentworth, with the aid of Ram Singh, dragged the iron bed into the living room and rolled it against the door. Other furniture, almost all of it, was next wedged against the door beside the staunch, iron bed.

Then Wentworth turned to Molly who was silently watching him with worshipful eyes. She did not seem frightened. There was only one thing which could frighten her, and that was her father's danger.

"We must get out of here, Molly," Wentworth said. "Are you willing to do what I say?"

She nodded her head eagerly. "Yes, anything!" And she meant it.

But Molly did not know what was going to happen to her. At Wentworth's request she sat upon the only chair which was not being used to barricade the door. Behind her Ram Singh stood with a pair of shears, and rapidly her fair curls fell to the floor, leaving her with hair of boyish length. The hair was cut a little raggedly as though it had been done at home by mother with a bowl. Ram Singh was an artist in matters of disguise.

Wentworth, watching the trembling of the barricaded door, gave Ram Singh further directions about Molly and let his servant work his skill upon her.

FROM THE closet of nondescript clothing, the Hindu selected a pair of ragged trousers and shortened the legs a full foot, with the same shears which had clipped the fair curls. Molly put on the trousers and a flannel shirt in the bedroom and returned to have the slack waist of the trousers drawn snug above her hips by means of a stout piece of twine. A torn coat, much too big, concealed the girlishness of her form from casual inspection; and a cloth cap, also too big, gave her the impish appearance of a gamin of the streets. But her complexion was too good and Ram Singh's agile fingers applied some traces of shoe blacking before Molly had really become a boy to all outward appearances.

So rapidly had Ram Singh worked that the transformation had only required a very few minutes. But even during that short time the barricade at the door had loosened perceptibly, and a heavy bar was being forced in at the back of the door to tear it from its hinges.

But Wentworth himself now took the chair in which Molly had sat, his pistol on his knee as he watched the door. Again Ram Singh went to work. The sticky hair was brushed violently before being treated with a subtle powder which left it white except for some gray streaks. A ragged, gray mustache was added to the upper lip, so skillfully that only a jerk could detect the fraud. The cheeks were smeared with a liquid from one of Ram Singh's tiny bottles, and they magically lost their freshness and became pallid and old. Eyebrows were touched by a tiny brush, and the hints of wrinkles were traced.

"You come out of that building.

What floor were you on?"

Richard Wentworth had become an old man. He drew on a long, black coat and placed a battered, felt hat upon his head. There was a tin cup in the pocket of the black coat, and around his neck Ram Singh hung a card marked "BLIND."

There only remained the adding of black patches over the eyes but although the black patches had pin holes, through which Wentworth could see fairly well, he did not consider it wise to impede his sight in the slightest until the last moment.

Molly Dennis, returning from the bathroom where she had been staring at her new self in the mirror, failed to recognize Wentworth until he spoke to her.

"And you, Ram Singh," directed Wentworth, "will go, when I leave here, to the Oriental Restaurant on Seventh Avenue. There you will lose yourself among the men from India until anybody, who may have followed you from here, has lost all trace of you."

"Han, sahib!" agreed Ram Singh with emphasis. "Boy go! Bad man no can find."

"Good boy!"

The Hindu boy's face glowed with pleasure, as it always did at the least compliment from his master.

"But how are we going to get out of here?" Molly asked, teetering from one foot to the other and looking down at her raggedly clothed legs.

"I'll show you," Wentworth answered and spoke rapidly to the Hindu in his own language, so that his meaning would be quite clear.

Ram Singh, blindly obedient, hurried into the closet and

returned with a great armful of the heterogeneous clothing which Wentworth used in his many disguises. He carried the clothes into the bathroom and dumped them into the bathtub. Again and again he returned to the closet and carried more and more clothes into the bathroom, where he dumped them, in a tumbled mass into the tub.

"And where are we going when we do get out of here?" asked Molly, very much puzzled by what Ram Singh was doing.

"My Dear Molly," returned Wentworth, smiling, "we are going back where we came from—back to Dan Grogan's Restaurant."

CHAPTER 5
FIRE!

THE IMPISH face of the make-believe street gamin showed sudden alarm at the mention of Grogan's Restaurant. After all, she was a girl—and she had been threatened with death in that restaurant only a few hours previously.

Wentworth watched her calculatingly. Much that he might do would depend upon her nerve and courage. Even in the presence of imminent danger, he so judged little things so that he might base his future actions upon them.

"If it's for father," she said, while the alarm left her face and was replaced by an attractive stubbornness, "I'll go there or anywhere else. I'd go to hell for him!"

"Good girl!" grinned Wentworth. "We'll go together."

It did not seem to strike Molly as strange that this man was doing so much for her father. His was a direct friendliness which reached her and gave her unquestioning confidence in him, even under the guise of the unattractive characters he was portraying. And there was nobody else in all the world who could do anything for her. She was quite certain of that, and she had to accept him without reason and without question.

She watched him as, with grayed hair and in his long, black coat, he stood calmly regarding the door, judging its remaining strength. With the intention of forcing the door outward into the hall, a crowbar was being inserted, high up near the top hinge.

In the bathroom Ram Singh had completed his task of piling the old clothes in the bathtub. The closet was empty and the tub held all the clothes in the apartment save those which were being worn by the three inmates.

Molly was puzzled. She did not understand the reason for this strange proceeding. Neither did Ram Singh understand it. But Ram Singh was only puzzled when he did not understand how to do what he was told to do. The reason for doing anything was his master's business and, since his master was always right, there could be no sense in worrying about it. It was a pleasant philosophy.

But the reason for the strange proceeding began to be made clear when Wentworth took from the shelf of the closet a large can of kerosene, an old-fashioned remedy which Ram Singh used upon rusty knife blades and gun barrels. Over the mass of clothes in the bathtub he poured the entire contents of the can.

Then he snapped his cigarette lighter and deliberately set fire to the mass.

Smoky, yellow flames rose from the tub as the mass of old clothes began to smolder and burn with sickly, soot laden flares. The smoke increased in volume, filled the bathroom and passed out through the open window to the street in a thick stream.

Wentworth closed the bathroom door and returned to the living room where Ram Singh watched the door, fingering his long knife. Molly came and stood beside her new-found protector. The two of them presented a curious spectacle, the tall, cadaverous man in the long, black coat and the saucy street urchin who was almost lost in the dilapidated trousers and loose-hanging coat.

Near the upper hinge of the door the biting end of the crowbar was being forced inward. It would not be long now before the proper leverage was obtained and the door wrenched bodily outward into the hall. Wentworth observed this, but apparently remained unmoved. Quietly he gave the Hindu some final instructions in his own language, to which Ram Singh replied at intervals with an emphatic. *"Han, sahib!"*—to indicate his perfect agreement and willingness to do what was wanted.

"Fire!" From somewhere in the building a woman could faintly be heard as she screamed that word of grim alarm. There are some buildings in New York where almost anything may be done without attracting the interest of other inmates; but there is no building in the entire world where the alarm of fire will not focus attention. The volume of smoke escaping from the bathroom window must have become quite prodigious.

Some of it was now seeping under the bathroom door and creeping into the living room.

Wentworth smiled. Even the underworld characters in the hall would be respectful to the danger of the attention which fire would draw from other people and ultimately from the New York Fire Department. New York firemen could be just as rough as New York policemen.

UNEXPECTEDLY THE smile died from Wentworth's face, and he asked Molly a question—a question which completely astonished her.

"Molly," he asked, "were you ever in love?"

Her face was not so boyish as she met the surprising question. A mixture of sorrow and anger flitted across it as she looked down at the floor without answering.

"Well, Molly," continued Wentworth, the smile returning to his face, "I see that you have a sweetheart but have quarreled with him."

Her cheeks reddened even through the grime which Ram Singh had implanted upon them. "How do you know that?" she demanded, the question admitting the truth of the statement he had made.

It was an extraordinary conversation under the circumstances. Even as he answered her the crowbar again splintered the door, and it was apparent that the attacking men had not yet become aware of the coming commotion.

"I couldn't tell you, Molly," he replied. "Women, and even little girls, are like pieces of old Chinese porcelain. A sixth sense is necessary to understand them. But tell me, who is this sweet-heart of yours?"

"Jerry Stone," she answered. "He was an assistant bookkeep-er under father in the Mack Syndicate."

Wentworth looked interested in what she said, but did not continue the conversation. The distant woman was again scream-ing "Fire!" and, outside the door, the men had ceased to wield the crowbar. No doubt they were waiting to see what was going to happen. Undoubtedly they were watching the door in case Wentworth should emerge.

But Wentworth seemed in no hurry to emerge or to take his next step. He appeared to be listening, and while he listened his mind sought some additional occupation—with the result that he picked up the telephone and dialed a number as casu-ally as if he had been at home in his own library with faithful old Jenkyns, the butler, at his beck and call.

And it was across New York that he sent his voice, high up into the tower of Riverside Mansions where the small apartment of Nita Van Sloan looked down upon the Hudson River far below. It was there that Nita, of the brown curls and blue eyes of mystery, lived with Apollo, the Great Dane dog that had been a gift from Richard Wentworth when a puppy.

Nita painted light effects upon the Hudson and sometimes sold them because her family and her fortune had been swept away by the war. Apollo adored Nita and was quite ready to be the bringer of sudden death to any enemy of hers.

"Nita, this is Dick," Wentworth commenced, and lapsed at once into the French language, although it was, perhaps, a trifle rude of him to use a language which he judged that Molly could not understand.

But Wentworth used the romantic language of France for the speech of love, and a man should be pardoned for speaking such words in private. In the midst of hard problems and during moments of action and danger, his mind always felt the stimulation of Nita's influence. At such times he frequently telephoned to her, sometimes from across the ocean, just to feel the stirring uplift which was carried to him by her voice.

And Nita knew the powerful stimulation which she could give him. Always she gave of herself to him wholeheartedly, although she was aware that his life was such that they probably never could be married. There was compensation, however, for her. She knew that she would never have cause for jealousy, and that is something which many a wife does not possess.

Molly watched him with her big Irish eyes, looking out from her grimy face, and, although she did not understand the words he used, she recognized the tone of his voice. And there was no secret from her in the message of his heart.

IN THE midst of the telephone conversation there came a clanging from the street. The New York Fire Department had sent some of its apparatus to the building which was allowing such a great quantity of black smoke to issue from one of its bathroom windows. Wentworth heard the fire gongs and suspended his telephone talk for a moment in order to issue some rapid directions to Ram Singh. Then he continued his conversation with Nita as quietly as if nothing at all were happening.

Ram Singh slipped his great knife into a sheath within his

sleeve, held a large handkerchief over his mouth and nose and rushed into the bathroom where he closed the window and returned to the living room, leaving the door open behind him.

The smoke, having its first exit closed, found the new exit immediately and began rolling into the living room. Ram Singh looked at the incoming smoke and transferred his gaze to his master, waiting for further directions.

Wentworth, however, continued to talk over the telephone quite as though volumes of smoke were perfectly natural to a living room. Molly began to cough a little. Ram Singh remained impassive, eyes fixed on Wentworth, waiting.

Presently as Ram Singh, at a motion from his master, began taking down the barricades from the door, Molly heard the telephone conversation turn back into the English language. She was so interested in what he said that she did not cough so much because of the smoke which was coming into the room.

Wentworth was talking about Mortimer Mack, President of the Mack Syndicate. He seemed to be asking Nita what she thought of him and how much she knew about him.

"Mortimer Mack brought a fairly good polish out of Harvard," Wentworth said, "but he's only on the fringe of society and still trying to get in. I'm on the trail of something, however, which may get him into Sing Sing before he gets into the Social Register. Suppose you and I go after him, Nita! Let's take him apart and see how he's put together. If he is all right, we will restore any missing parts. What say?"

While Wentworth was listening to Nita's reply, Molly was crouching near the floor with a handkerchief over her nose, trying to keep from coughing on account of the smoke, which was becoming more and more dense. Ram Singh had taken the last of the barricade away from the door and stood with his hand on the bolt, looking back at his master.

Molly, gasping, also looked back at Wentworth and wondered how he managed to refrain from coughing. He seemed so calm and at his ease as he sat at the telephone in the smoke.

She began to believe that he must be superhuman. What other kind of a man would and could do the things for her that he was doing? She did not wonder so much about Ram Singh. She had heard that Hindus could walk on fire with bare feet and, if they could do that, they could probably breathe smoke quite easily. As for herself, she could not help coughing. But she would die before she would complain.

Through the rolling smoke Molly could see Wentworth adjusting the black patches over his eyes. She did not know that each black patch had a tiny pinhole which gave him considerable vision. Suddenly she realized that she would have to lead him through the streets of the city—if they ever got out of the building.

Heavy steps sounded on the stairs. The firemen were coming up.

Wentworth rose to his feet with the telephone in his hand, still talking.

"I am afraid I shall have to ring off," he said. "I have an engagement to take a young lady out to a restaurant."

He replaced the telephone upon the table and came forward,

holding out his hand for Molly. She grasped it eagerly, fear-lessly.

"Open the door," he said to Ram Singh.

CHAPTER 6
THE DISAPPEARING SAFE

RAM SINGH drew back the bolt and threw the door open. Out into the hall swirled the smoke from the room. For a moment all three stood perfectly still, breathing as little as possible.

From the doorway nobody could be seen in the hall. But there came a burst of excited voices from some little distance away, as the smoke swept out; and directions could be heard from firemen on the stairs.

Wentworth reached with his free hand and tapped Ram Singh on the shoulder. Instantly the Hindu slipped into the hall and darted toward the rear of the building, his business being to lose himself amid the smoke and shadows and among the excited people who always assemble at the alarm of fire. Later, when he was quite certain that he had not been followed, he would rejoin his master in his surroundings utterly different from those which he had just left behind him.

It was just possible, of course, that he might meet an enemy of his master. But it was not likely, since the attacking men were almost certainly unaware that a Hindu had been in the apartment they were trying to enter. In any case Ram Singh, with the long knife up his sleeve, was not a good man to attack.

51

Wentworth hesitated a few seconds longer, listening to the sounds of the firemen on the stairs and judging their nearness. Then he seized Molly's arm above the elbow and together they passed out into the hall, turning amid the smoke toward the head of the stairs upon which firemen were in the act of bringing up a line of hose.

So far as he could see through the pinholes in his black eye-patches there was no sign of his enemies. There were some open doors through which peered the frightened faces of inmates who were aroused by the dread alarm of fire, and at the head of the stairs a fireman with an ax was just stepping onto the landing.

"Hey, Bill!" shouted the fireman. "Here's a blind man. See that he doesn't trip over the hose."

Wentworth and Molly, old blind man and young street urchin, passed down the stairs slowly and listened to the talk of the ascending firemen. It was some kind of an unusual smoker, the firemen thought, and didn't have any real heat. They were professionally callous about the fire but gave kindly attention to the blind man. There were still no signs of the men who had been trying to force their way into the apartment. But it was in the street that Wentworth expected to find them, if he found them at all at the scene of the fire.

Outside the entrance to the building a couple of policemen were driving back a small crowd of onlookers and it was into this crowd that Wentworth and Molly found their way. Molly was apparently leading the tall man at her side. But in reality Wentworth was guiding her by means of the firm hold which he maintained upon her arm. Yet he stumbled a little and bumped into some people just as he might have done if she had really been leading him.

On the outside of the crowd, well back from the police, stood a man whom Wentworth recognized instantly. He was the man with the patent leather shoes who had worn the policeman's uniform. He was wearing another coat now, but the policeman's uniform probably reposed in a paper-covered bundle under his arm. Wentworth edged away from this man, directing Molly down the street toward a subway station. But the man noticed them and caught up to them.

"You come out of that building?" he asked. "What floor were you on?"

"Eh?" asked Wentworth, moving on, apparently under the influence of his small companion.

"He's deaf," said Molly.

The man, whose question had been rather listless, turned away. Few care to talk with a deaf person, especially when the questions have to be shouted so that others may hear them.

"That was clever of you to tell him that I was deaf," said Wentworth as they continued slowly toward the subway. "If you do it again, however, call if 'deef.' It will fit your character better."

But Wentworth regretted the meeting with the man who had posed as a policeman. Should he meet him again, while posing as the blind man, the fellow would probably become suspicious.

THEY TOOK the subway to Grand Central Station, shuttled from there to Times Square and traveled north on the west side of Manhattan as far as 96th Street before taking a southbound local which would carry them into the neighborhood of Grogan's Restaurant. Wentworth's purpose was to use up a little time and to make doubly certain that he was not being followed.

As they traveled Wentworth instructed the girl, even going to the extreme of making her pretend to guide him as he passed along the aisle of the subway train with his little tin cup held out in a trembling hand. Several passengers dropped pennies into the cup, and one old lady parted with a dime. By the time that they reached their destination Molly had become quite expert in obeying the slightest pressure that Wentworth placed upon her arm.

Half a block from Grogan's Restaurant they passed a blue car which was parked by the curb. It was empty, but Wentworth noticed that the back bumper was badly bent as if it had been in a severe collision. It seemed that Grogan had returned to his restaurant.

A police department car was parked in front of the place, and people were still stopping in the street to peer through the front window. But business was again going on as usual in Grogan's Restaurant. New York City does little more than hesitate for such a thing as sudden death. The police act swiftly in the business section, and the dead are soon carried away to be dealt with in legal routine beyond the public eye.

Wentworth, with Molly slightly in advance of him, turned boldly into the restaurant, stumbled slightly on the step and fumbled with a chair at an empty table, a chair which faced the door of the little back room. There were two waiters in Grogan's Restaurant at night, most of the business being done then. One of these came forward and bluntly said that panhandlers were not wanted. But he accepted an order for coffee and beans when Wentworth took some silver from his pocket and exposed it in his trembling hand. All kinds of unfashionable people came to Grogan's Restaurant and were welcomed if they had money to pay for what they wanted.

Wentworth leaned back in his chair and remained quite motionless, as if he were tired, while he waited for the coffee and beans. Through the pinholes in the black patches over his eyes, however, he could see the door of the back room. Several men, evidently detectives in plain clothes, passed in and out of the room, sometimes going into the kitchen, sometimes passing out to the street and sometimes using a telephone booth which was built against the wall which separated the restaurant from the back room.

Presently Dan Grogan himself came out of the back room and stood looking around his cheap little eating place. He seemed to be very angry, and he made no effort to conceal it. He was probably annoyed by the questions of the police, and he was certainly angry because of what had been done in his little back room after he had left it late that afternoon. Possibly he had already discovered that something had been taken from his iron safe.

Grogan came to the front of the restaurant and stood in his customary place beside the battered cash register. He gave but a cursory glance at the blind man and ragged boy before biting the end off a fresh cigar and commencing to chew it. As he stood there, only four or five feet from Wentworth, a man entered and stood quietly beside him. Wentworth did not dare turn his head to focus his pinholes upon the newcomer, but he was close enough to hear the conversation.

"Did the bulls blow yet?" asked the newcomer.

"Naw!" Grogan answered in disgust. They just found the gat that did the killing. It was in the waste basket, and a piece of paper fell on it. Can you beat it? Some bulls! The photographer is coming back to take the finger prints off it." Grogan spat some of his cigar on the floor. "Hell of a lot of good it's going to do them!"

"Why isn't it going to do them any good?"

Grogan's only answer was to spit some more of his cigar upon the floor. His companion seemed to take it as a hint that there was to be no more talk and slipped quietly out of the restaurant. Grogan turned his back and stared morosely out into the street.

What Wentworth had heard gave him much uneasiness. It seemed certain that his pistol must have fallen out of its holster when he had stooped to pick up Molly. If it was one that was registered with the police, and he was almost certain that it was, it would certainly be traced to him. Even if, by chance, he had not left distinct finger prints upon it, there would be exceedingly awkward questions to answer.

But Wentworth did not remain uneasy very long. A tight corner only made life more interesting for him.

In all probability his pistol was merely waiting for him to come and get it. The problem of getting it was a hard one, but that was the only kind of a problem that really interested him. While Molly played with the toothpicks upon the table, he viewed the situation calmly, took stock of all his surroundings and commenced to make his plans.

A DETECTIVE came out of the back room and entered the telephone booth. Wentworth wondered if there were other detectives in that little room. The detective had left the door open, but Wentworth could see only a part of the room beyond.

Then it was that Wentworth saw something that gave him a very great surprise. Through the open door he found himself looking at the iron safe, and he was pleased with himself for having so carefully wiped his finger prints from the dial after opening it to impress Grogan with his skill.

As he gazed, he saw the black handle which is used to swing open the door after working the combination. Black? He remembered that the handle on the safe door, which he had opened, had had a bright nickel covering. He was certain of that; yet he now saw a black handle. He looked more closely at the safe, and slowly he became convinced that he was not looking at the same safe that had been there late that afternoon!

The thing seemed to be an impossibility. Yet it was undoubtedly so. The safe had been taken away and another safe put in its place. Certainly the room had been unguarded by the police for only a few minutes, a very few minutes, after he had rushed out of it with Molly in his arms. It did not seem possible that so heavy a thing could have been spirited away in the twinkling of an eye. Yet in no other way could it have been done unless, of course, it had been done with the connivance of the police, which Wentworth could not believe. Here was a mystery which he would have to solve if it took him the rest of his life.

The waiter came with the coffee and beans, and Molly stopped playing with the toothpicks. She was really very hungry. As for Wentworth, he could not play his role of an old and rather sickly blind man if he ate too ravenously. Besides, he intended to enter the little back room before the beans were finished. He leaned forward and spoke in a very low voice so that only Molly could hear.

Molly played her part quite well. She rose slowly, reluctant to leave her supper, and guided the old blind man across the room to the telephone booth where she placed a nickel in the slot and dialed for him since, of course, it would be strange if a blind man could do such a thing for himself. No sooner had she finished dialing and handed him the receiver than she scurried back to her plate of beans as if they were much more important than her guardianship of the old man.

In the telephone booth Wentworth pulled down the hook to break the connection, but held the receiver to his ear for the benefit of any person who might look in through the glass door. He remained in this position for some two or three minutes, while Molly, following instruction, gobbled her beans and paid no attention to him.

The girl was still eating when Wentworth opened the door of the booth and groped his way out. He felt before him with his hands and touched the wall. Two or three steps brought him to the door of the little back room and his hand fell on the knob as if by accident. The door opened and he staggered into the room with hands outstretched as a blind man might be expected to do if he had lost his bearings.

Wentworth could see quite a bit although, of course, he could not see perfectly. He was able to see the detective sitting by the desk. He glimpsed the iron safe. He just had time to see a pistol lying upon the desk, when the detective rose from his chair.

"What the hell?" was the detective's remark, an expression of surprise rather than a question.

Wentworth swayed before the detective and his knees shook. "Water!" he gasped and seemed to have difficulty in breathing.

A New York policeman is supposed to be a very hardened individual. But in the case of a poor old blind man, struggling to breathe, he is apt to be quite soft-hearted. The detective helped Wentworth into the chair from which he himself had just risen and rushed out into the restaurant to pour a glass of water from a water bottle.

AS THE detective rushed away, Wentworth picked up the pistol from the desk and stowed it away in a pocket with the speed of lightning. He slid out of the chair to the floor, apparently in agony, and robed over to the safe, with two objects in view. In the first place he wanted to get as far away from the desk as possible so that the detective, upon returning, would not be so likely to look at the place which had been occupied by the pistol. In the second place he wanted to examine the floor underneath the mat upon which the safe rested.

In the few seconds which elapsed before the return of the detective Wentworth proved to his own satisfaction the only theory which he had been able to deduce to explain the mystery of the vanishing safe. He slipped his fingers underneath the edge of the mat and found, as he had suspected, that the floor, had been cut. The safe was really resting upon a platform which could be made to sink into the basement where, no doubt, it could be shifted by some mechanism, and another safe sent up in its place. The edges of the mat covered the cutting in the floor, but could be folded up and passed through the aperture when the safe was lowered. And this was the trick which Grogan used to deceive the police upon their occasional inspection.

But between the detective's legs, as he came back through the door, Wentworth saw an awkward, if not dangerous, situation arising in the restaurant. The man with the patent leather shoes, who had posed as a policeman, was just entering the restaurant.

"Here you are!" exclaimed the detective, closing the door and cutting off Wentworth's view of the restaurant as he came in. "Drink this!"

Wentworth raised his head and sipped the water which the detective gave him. Outside he heard Molly scream, one short, frightened cry. He struggled to his feet, spilled the water over the detective's knee and rushed gropingly toward the door, throwing it open and staggering into the restaurant.

Quick as he was, he was too late. Molly was not in the restaurant, and the bogus policeman also had disappeared. Through the restaurant he staggered, upsetting chairs, until he passed through the front door into the street, the astonished detective watching him from behind. His acting was perfect, but probably he would have met an obstruction in big Dan

Grogan if it had not been for the immediate presence of the detective.

Nor was there any sign of Molly in the street. Wentworth was so troubled about her that he tore off the black patches which covered his eyes and cast discretion to the winds. There was nothing that he could do until he had got rid of the disguise he was wearing, a disguise which was now useless in that district.

He jumped upon the running board of a passing taxi and was out of sight of Grogan's Restaurant in a few seconds.

But there was more surprise for Wentworth that evening. In the light of the taxi he examined the pistol which he had snatched from beneath the detective's nose.

The pistol was not his!

CHAPTER 7
MASTER OF SEVEN
MILLION PEOPLE!

I T WAS just before dinner on the following evening that Ram Singh finally returned to Wentworth's Park Avenue apartment. His first act was to light some incense and place it before old Ganesh the elephant-headed god of India—the god which he had carefully brought away from the apartment which they had deserted. In his own room he squatted upon the floor while the incense burned and chanted a mantra in a low voice. Ganesh was a god who should be carefully cultivated if good luck were to remain with Ram Singh and with Ram Singh's master. And good luck was something to be greatly desired in

NITA VAN SLOAN

the adventurous life they both led.

His next act was to clothe himself completely in white, even as he would have done in his native land. His feet were made bare, and a great, white turban was bound about his head. Although American custom was quite the reverse Ram Singh always honored his master, in his own household, by baring his feet and covering his head. And of course this was done after proper ablutions which, to the Hindu, are quite as religious as they are cleansing.

It was in Wentworth's own bedroom that the Hindu boy found his master.

"*Sahib*, boy come!" was the succinct greeting, spoken in a very matter-of-fact tone as though they had not separated under alarming circumstances.

"Good boy!" was the

equally short acknowledgment of the greeting, spoken with warmth. But there was a frown upon his master's face.

Something was wrong. Ram Singh had long since learned to read his master's face, perhaps because his master trusted him so much that he never tried to hide things from him.

"Molly, *missie sahib?*" the boy suddenly asked. "She not get hurt?"

Wentworth's frown deepened and he walked out of the room in a deep study without replying.

Ram Singh waited in the bedroom to dress his master for dinner. He laid out the fresh shirt and clothes upon the bed so reverentially and methodically as almost to make it appear a rite. But Wentworth did not return.

Presently the boy heard his

RICHARD WENTWORTH

63

master's violin from the music room. The music was wild, tempestuous and angry. Ram Singh understood that music. He knew that it reflected the mind of the man who was playing the violin. He continued to wait and heard Jenkyns, the butler, pass along the corridor to announce dinner.

Ram Singh replaced his master's evening clothes with a solemn face. The angry tones of the violin were indication that something was wrong. The fact that his master did not dress for dinner indicated something very close to a tragedy. In all his experience Ram Singh could not remember an occasion when his master did not dress for dinner—when dressing was possible.

Back to his own bedroom went the Hindu servant to sharpen his long knife and to burn more incense before the squat figure of old Ganesh.

And in the big dining room at the huge, round table sat Wentworth alone. Jenkyns, too, was surprised that his master had not dressed for dinner, but he served with impassive face and careful attention which was the result of long training. In the middle of it he was called to the telephone and returned with a portable telephone which he plugged into the wall and handed to Wentworth where he sat.

IT WAS Wentworth's old friend, Ned Morris, who was calling. "Hello, Dick old man!" he exclaimed. "I saw Mortimer Mack and he said he would be glad to have you come over tonight and by all means to bring any lady you wished."

"Thanks, old chap! I have heard something about Mortimer Mack's entertainments. What kind of a crowd will be there?"

"Oh, frightfully mixed, but there will be some nice people. By the way, you had better take your check book."

"Oh, is it that kind of a party?"

"Yes, but it's not what you think, and you will be surprised. It's a gorgeous entertainment. By all means go and have a look at it. I can't make the man out myself."

Wentworth handed the telephone back to Jenkyns and finished his dinner much more heartily than he had commenced it.

After dinner he telephoned Nita. "We are going out to take Mortimer Mack to pieces," he said. "Are you game? I'll call for you about eleven. Wear something smart to impress the old codger."

Nita laughed her rippling, throaty laugh. "How will a Chanel black satin dress with a pink satin yoke do?" she asked. "There are black ostrich cuffs and a tiny boa—quite a fantasy."

"Sounds all right," replied Wentworth, "and I'll bet that it will look all right—with you inside it."

After dinner Wentworth, when he was alone, usually spent some time in the library with coffee and liqueurs. But tonight he dispensed with the coffee and liqueurs and returned to the music room. Once more the sound of his violin was heard. But the music was no longer angry and tempestuous. It was spirited, but it was also romantic. There was some kind of action ahead of him—and he was going out with Nita.

Ram Singh heard the music again and noticed the change in it. He sensed action of some kind. Well, he was ready. The point of his knife was very sharp and enough incense had been burned before old Ganesh to ward off much danger. Later, although disappointed that he was to be left behind, he performed the rite of dressing his master with extreme care.

Tonight Wentworth was wearing full evening dress, and there was no blue cornflower for Ram Singh to adjust in the buttonhole as he always did when a dinner jacket was worn. Neither was there to be any white gardenia. Wentworth was wearing the rosette of the Legion of Honor, and he never wore a flower when he wore a decoration.

Ram Singh gazed in admiration when his work was done. But he noticed that his master was not taking with him any pistol or weapon of other description. As a matter of fact, a pistol cannot be carried in full evening dress without marring the effect of the clothes.

NITA VAN SLOAN dressed very carefully to go out with Richard Wentworth that night, for she regarded him above all other men. Their attachment was something complete; yet it might never reach culmination in marriage. A man should not marry if he is apt to meet sudden death at any moment. Certainly he should not marry if there is a chance that he may be sent to prison or the electric chair.

As Nita stood before her mirror, after dressing, she thought of this, and there was a wistful expression upon her face for a moment. But it was only for a moment. Tonight she was going out with Dick, and that was sufficient. She was very smart in the Chanel gown, one of her few extravagances. In her middle twenties she still possessed the abandon and charm of the subdeb and added to those qualities the attraction which can come only to a woman who has experienced life.

The war and the financial crash of 1929 had swept away Nita's family and almost all of her fortune, but she still remained a Van Sloan, a member of that family which had come to America so long ago and which had remained in the forefront of New York society ever since.

Nita and Apollo, the Great Dane, were standing by the window of her tower apartment on Riverside Drive, looking down on the misty Hudson River, when Wentworth arrived. Both the girl and the dog, in their different ways, welcomed him as only those who love can do.

"Let's sit here and look down at the river for a while," Nita suggested. "Dick, you are looking a little bit worried. Is it that Molly girl that you told me about over the telephone?"

Wentworth's face clouded perceptibly. "Yes," he admitted. "I may have been the cause of her death."

"You forget that they would have killed her if you had not interfered in the first place," Nita returned. "But I am sorry, and I wish we could do something."

"Sooner or later I shall do something," he answered emphatically. "If I fail to save her life, I can at least avenge her death."

"Do you really think that Mortimer Mack is mixed up in it?" she asked.

From his pocket Wentworth took a little, black book and handed it to her. It was the only thing of importance which he had found among the papers which he had so hastily crammed into his pockets when he had robbed Dan Grogan's iron safe just before he had rushed out of the restaurant with poor little Molly in his arms.

The first page of the book was headed "Mack's List." There followed a long list of names and addresses. Some of the names had crosses after them, and some names were marked O.K.

"You are looking at a list of names," explained Wentworth as Nita studied the book in puzzlement, "which includes all of the most important politicians of New York City."

"Well?" Nita was still puzzled.

"Notice the names which are marked with a cross," he continued. "Each of those men is dead, or is in a sanitarium, or has mysteriously vanished from sight! Those in sanitariums are there because they have become drug addicts. The dead are believed to have been murdered or to have committed suicide. I have made inquiries, and that is the astounding truth."

Nita stared in amazement at the list in her hand.

"Even I can see that there is something horrid going on," she said. "Whatever does it mean?"

He explained to her how he had come into possession of the little black book and he told her what he had learned from Molly about the secret connection between the notorious Dan Grogan and the Mack Syndicate.

In addition he had made inquiries through his banker and through his lawyer about Mortimer Mack and his wealthy syndicate. It was reported to him on good authority that Mortimer Mack was worth many millions and that he was becoming more and more wealthy by leaps and bounds, through city contracts which he seemed to win from all other competitors in some mysterious way.

"But I don't yet see just what is being done and how and why," Nita protested. "If this were a list of city officials, I would suppose that some kind of an attack were being made upon them to force them to favor the Mack Syndicate."

Wentworth smiled. "Don't you know," he asked, "that the politicians govern the city officials? Nita, the man who rules the politicians—rules New York City!"

"Oh!" she gasped. "And do you think that Mortimer Mack is actually trying to gain control of the great city of New York?"

"Yes," he answered quietly, "I do. I believe that Mortimer Mack, or someone above him, is to a large extent already in control of New York. I believe that he gets the politicians into his power by means of dope and women and, perhaps, by means of gambling. When he fails to control a politician I believe that he has that politician murdered or cause him to commit suicide by bringing ruin or disgrace to him."

"Dick, it's shocking!" Nita exclaimed "It's disgusting and horrible to think that such a man can enslave seven million people like that!"

Suddenly Wentworth grinned as if he had not a care in the world.

"But think what fun we'll have in taking old Mortimer Mack to pieces," he said. "Ready? Let's go!"

CHAPTER 8
MORTIMER MACK'S PLACE

I T WAS nearly midnight when Richard Wentworth's town car swooped, slowed and stilled itself before the huge Fifth Avenue apartment house in which Mortimer Mack had his residence. The immense building was New York's latest word in residential luxury. Rentals were staggering and were not even mentioned publicly. Door men were gazed at in awe by people from the tops of passing buses. The place was considered to be a trifle vulgar by members of New York's old society *régime* but many of them, impoverished by changing conditions, would have been glad to live there.

Wentworth, assisting Nita to alight from his car, was pushed by a newsboy, shouting a late extra.

"All about th' Spider murder!" the boy shouted. New clue found! Arrest soon!"

Nita heard the newsboy and stumbled a little in getting out of the car. In all the world she was the only person who knew about the Spider. She alone possessed Wentworth's secret.

Her hand trembled on his arm as they left the car. Dick Wentworth was in great danger if the newspaper report were true.

But Wentworth showed no sign of alarm and did not even appear to hear the newsboy. He escorted Nita through the ornate doors and across the gorgeous hall as unconcernedly as if he had been strolling with her along some country lane. They were a very attractive couple, and even the hall men turned their eyes a trifle while they stood stiffly at their stations.

"Jolly little place!" remarked Wentworth jocularly. Then, more seriously: "But don't forget that murder and sudden death can occur in such a place."

Mortimer Mack's apartment proved to be duplex. From a spacious hall a broad, curved stairway led to the second floor. The hall was really very large, but seemed even larger than it actually was because the walls were completely paneled with mirrors. In addition to the stairway there was an automatic elevator for those who might be infirm or, perhaps, a bit drunk. In every way the apartment gave the appearance of a house, as in truth it was—a very large house, with many rooms—constructed within the apartment building.

Wentworth had given his name upon entering. He noticed that the servant paid particular attention to it and immediately sent another servant upon some errand. Evidently somebody was being notified of his arrival, perhaps the owner of the establishment himself.

And such proved to be the case. Wentworth had returned from the men's coat room and was waiting for Nita in the mirror-lined hall when she was approached by a small man with beetling eyebrows and iron-gray hair, a man with a soft voice and cold, shrewd eyes.

"Mr. Wentworth, I am Mortimer Mack," the man said softly. "Mr. Morris said you were coming, and I'm so glad you could do so. I met you once at a polo game several years ago, but I'm afraid you have forgotten me."

71

"Glad to be here," returned Wentworth briefly. "Ned Morris here?"

"He is upstairs somewhere," Mortimer Mack replied. "I would like to have a talk with you later. In the meantime, won't you make yourself perfectly at home?"

The soft voice ceased and the man seemed to drift away and disappear with a certain, curious ease which was heightened by his reflections in the many mirrors. His disappearance was really quite simple. He entered the automatic elevator and abruptly cut himself off from sight by closing its mirror-covered door. Although his manner had been quite normal there was, nevertheless, a strange atmosphere of cold cruelty about him. He gave the feeling that he would quietly go to any extreme to achieve his own objectives.

NITA JOINED Wentworth a moment later. Together they ascended the stairs and were attracted to a large ballroom where an orchestra was dispensing music for those who wanted to dance. At her suggestion they drifted out upon the floor and danced while they studied the people about them.

As they danced, Wentworth recognized a prominent politician who was dancing, and not any too well, with an extremely beautiful woman who wore a dress of emerald green, cut so daringly as to cause many of the men to annoy their partners by turning their heads in her direction. It was common knowledge that this man had a very quiet little wife and several children. Wentworth wondered what the quiet wife thought about the lady in emerald green.

There might be other politicians present. Wentworth would

be unable to recognize most of them and none of them did he know personally. There were several very daring women on the floor, dancing with men he knew nothing about. Wentworth wondered about it and wondered, too, why he had not yet seen his friend, Ned Morris.

Neither could Wentworth understand why Ned Morris had advised him to bring his check book. The guests were busy in the refreshment rooms, upon the dance floor and at bridge in some card rooms. But the bridge seemed to be quite ordinary and nothing that would require any special hint regarding the bringing of a check book. Wentworth was beginning to think that the entertainment was quite tame when Nita gave him a surprise.

"Poor old Jerry Stone!" she exclaimed. "His partner got rid of him, just as I overheard her saying she would do in the dressing room."

"Jerry Stone!" exclaimed Wentworth. "Where is he?"

"Leaning against the pillar at the entrance to the ballroom and looking very bored and ill at ease," she answered.

Wentworth stopped dancing and walked around the edge of the ballroom with Nita toward the young man she had indicated. Jerry Stone was the name of the young man mentioned by poor little Molly during the exciting moments of the fire ruse—the young man who had been an assistant bookkeeper for the Mack Syndicate under her father.

Was it possible that this was that man? If so, it was strong evidence that something was not right in the Mack organization. Presidents of great companies do not invite assistant bookkeepers into their homes; and most certainly Mortimer Mack did not seem to be the kind of a man who would do such a thing unless there were some very special reason for it.

As they approached the young man it became quite plain that Nita was right in saying that he was ill at ease.

"A little warm to dance, don't you think?" commented Wentworth to the obviously uncomfortable young man, halting beside him with Nita. "My name is Wentworth. Didn't I meet you in Monte Carlo last year?"

The young man, even if ill at ease, was distinctly flattered by being addressed by so distinguished a man as Wentworth. He had never been outside of America, but the suggestion that he had been a visitor at such a place as Monte Carlo flattered him still more. He gave his name as Stone, but confessed that he had not been in Monte Carlo last year.

"Some other place, then," returned Wentworth carelessly. "I know I met you somewhere. Perhaps it was London. By the way, old man, who is the lady in emerald green, the one with the corking figure who is dancing with the fellow who can't dance?"

"Oh, ah, that's Cora," Stone replied, confused and embarrassed.

"Know 'em by their first names, eh?" Wentworth smiled understandingly. He looked at Nita, and she understood.

"Dance?" she said. "My partner is tired."

Jerry Stone blushed and hesitated, as Nita moved toward him. Then he danced away with her and Wentworth smiled ever so slightly, knowing that a clever woman can get much more information out of a man than can be obtained by another man.

WENTWORTH DECIDED that in the meantime he would return to the bottom floor of the duplex apartment for a sandwich, a glass of champagne and a look around. Two men, quite able bodied and sober, entered the automatic elevator as he came to the head of the curving stairway. He descended the stairs quite rapidly, but found that the elevator had beaten him. Either that or the car had not come down to this floor. He knew that automatic elevators are not noted for their speed, and the thing puzzled him. He was also puzzled about the whereabouts of his friend, Ned Morris. It was very strange that he had not yet caught a glimpse of him.

After a hurried glass of wine and a sandwich Wentworth went over to the automatic elevator and pressed the call button. Nobody paid any attention to him and very shortly the door opened and exposed the empty car. He entered and closed the door behind him. There were only two buttons to be pressed, one for the first floor and one for the second floor, which was what he expected.

As he was about to press the second button, with the intention of returning to the ballroom where Nita was dancing, the car started unexpectedly without his causing it to do so. Then Wentworth realized that there was more to the Mortimer Mack establishment than he had guessed. The car had started forward! Somebody had called it before he had time to press the button and the car was now bound for a floor for which there was no visible button in the car.

There was a stop button which Wentworth could have used, after which he could have sent the car up again. But it was not in his character to draw back or to hesitate when adventure beckoned. He had no idea how far down the car would go, or what he would find when it stopped. But he would go there and he would find what there was to be found.

He did not have long to wait. Very quickly the elevator stopped at what was, undoubtedly, one floor below the duplex apartment of Mortimer Mack. Or was it really a triplex apartment or even a quadplex apartment? Wentworth had no time to consider such possibilities before the door of the elevator opened.

Before him stood the woman called Cora, she of the emerald green gown which was cut so daringly and which fitted so snugly. And behind Cora was Dan Grogan!

CHAPTER 9
THE WOMAN CALLED CORA

RICHARD WENTWORTH would long since have been dead if his mind had not been capable of working with the speed of light. As the door of the elevator opened, exposing Cora and Dan Grogan, he knew that he had penetrated one of Mortimer Mack's secrets. And uncovering the secrets of such a man would no doubt prove dangerous business.

Twice before Wentworth had met Dan Grogan; once when he was posing as the underworld character with the plastered hair and the high-waisted trousers; and once as an old blind man in a long, black coat. In his real character, dressed in evening clothes from Bond Street, he did not believe that Grogan could recognize him. As for Cora, well, Wentworth knew all kinds of women.

So much he knew and considered in the split second before he acted. Then he hiccuped.

It was not a violent hiccup, just a modest little effort, which was scarcely big enough to be noticed. Wentworth pretended not to have noticed it himself. He swayed a little and commenced to speak.

"Call taxi?" he asked, looking at Grogan and again swaying slightly. "Lost my hat. No matter."

His speech was that of the man who curtails his words when under the influence of drink, but who is able to enunciate up to the point of going blotto.

It was Cora who first found her wits. "Leave him to me," she said. "He'll never know where he's been."

She stepped quickly into the elevator and closed the door upon Grogan's scowling face. Cora was one of those women who are super abundantly supplied with the knowledge of men. Although her action had been for the purpose of removing Wentworth as quickly as possible, she nevertheless recognized in him the type of man who might be exceedingly profitable to her. She pressed the first button and the car started upward.

Wentworth reached out a hand and pressed the stop button, bringing the car to a halt midway between floors "Don't want to go home now," he said.

"Well, where do you want to go?" she asked, smiling and

BUCKLEY

DAVID BANNISTER

CORA

leaning her green-clad figure against the side of the car opposite to him.

"No place," he answered. "Stay here forever."

She laughed, understanding his meaning and quite pleased by it. "We can't do that," she returned. "Somebody else might want to use this car."

"Then let's go Bermuda," he said. "Buy elevator there just for us."

She looked at him calculatingly. "You got a yacht?"

He looked depressed. "Yacht very vulgar. Let's go horseback.

JERRY STONE

MORTIMER MACK

DAN GROGAN

Get nice sea horse. Gods drive it."

Cora didn't know anything about the gods who drove sea horses. She pressed the first button again and the car commenced to rise. "You're crazy," she said.

They got out on the first floor of the duplex apartment and Wentworth insisted upon taking her into the dining room for a drink. Under in-structions from Cora, and it was very decent of her, the waiter brought Wentworth a bromo seltzer which he drank and told her that it was the best gin fizz he had ever tasted except that it was just a trifle weak.

"Let's go dance," he said when he had set down his glass.

"Can't," she replied. "Wish I could, but I have another engagement and I'm late now."

"Must dance," he insisted, taking her by the arm and leading her up the stairs. "After dance we'll get sea horse and gallop to Bermuda and never come back."

AND THEY did dance. She was an excellent dancer and he danced superbly, just as he fenced, shot, rode and swam. He told her that the gin fizz had gone to his feet, and she remembered that some drunken men can dance better than they can walk or talk. In five minutes they were Dick and Cora to each other. But she gave him little information about the Mortimer Mack establishment, and he forebore to put any direct questions. She did, however, hint that there was big gambling to be had and seemed rather surprised that he did not know about it. Once he touched on the subject of dope, and she seemed to show interest but did not pursue the subject.

Then, suddenly, Wentworth saw the politician with whom Cora had formerly been dancing, bearing down upon them from the other side of the ballroom. The politician's face was angry and his feet were not quite steady. And it was quite evident that he was going to cut in. At almost that same moment Wentworth caught sight of Nita talking to Mortimer Mack near the entrance to the ballroom. The little man's beetling eyebrows were dancing up and down, and he seemed animated as if he were quite enjoying the conversation. Wentworth decided to find out what was going on, and accordingly steered his partner straight into the angry politician, who took her over almost hungrily, like a big trout after a fat fly. Cora most certainly had that politician entangled in her meshes.

Wentworth was curious to know what Nita had done with Jerry Stone.

He was half way across the ballroom when Nita and her companion turned away and walked into the hall. He quickened his steps and reached the hall just in time to see the two of them entering the elevator. The door of the elevator closed, and the small, red light was extinguished, indicating that the car was in motion. Wentworth was just a little bit angry and just a little bit uneasy. Mack was probably taking Nita downstairs for some refreshment. It was that, or—

But Wentworth did not want to think of anything else.

He descended the curving stairs more rapidly than he believed it possible for the slow-moving elevator to reach the floor below. At the bottom of the stairs he waited, watching the door which opened upon the elevator shaft. The shaft was entirely enclosed, so that the elevator, whether in motion or stationary, was quite hidden until the door was opened. He waited several seconds anxiously and, for half a minute longer, in blank dismay.

But the door of the elevator remained shut and the elevator did not arrive.

Richard Wentworth was a man who could face his own death calmly. He could watch the death of another, if that death were necessary or unavoidable, quite as calmly. But the reverse was true—where Nita Van Sloan was concerned. Now he was calm in outward appearance only. He believed that she had been taken to the apartment below. And he could think of no reason why she should be taken there, except for purposes harmful to her.

THERE WERE several courses which he might pursue. He might break open the little door, climb down the shaft and force his way into the apartment below. He might go out into the big apartment building, descend to the lower floor and force his way into the same apartment through its outer door. And as a last resort, he might, call in the police. That course would be awkward, and he believed, too, that he could do more than they and do it more quickly.

He called a servant to him. "Where is Mr. Mack?" he asked.

"I do not know, sir."

"Tell him that Mr. Richard Wentworth sends his compliments and wishes to see him immediately."

"Very good, sir."

The servants seemed to be well trained. The man departed to look through the rooms and shortly afterward ascended the stairs to the floor above. Wentworth watched to see if he took the elevator, determined to accompany him, if possible, in that event. But he lost sight of the servant in the crowd on the floor above and, in his impatience, went to the elevator and pushed the call button himself. He would stop the car with the stop button half way between floors and tear the inside out of it until he had discovered the means of sending it to the secret apartment in which he had seen Dan Grogan.

There was some delay before the car arrived. But when it did so, there was another surprise for Wentworth. For out of the car stepped his friend, Ned Morris.

"Hello, Dick!" he exclaimed. "Nita sent me to get you."

"Nita? Is she all right?"

"Of course! Why the devil shouldn't she be?"

A smile broke over Wentworth's face. "Well, then," he asked, "where the devil is she?"

Ned Morris grinned. "I forgot that you had not been initiated," he said.

"Initiated?"

Ned Morris nodded. "There is more to this damned place than is to be seen at first glance," he explained.

Wentworth was on the point of saying that he had discovered that much. But long habit caused him to resist and to accept information rather than to give it even with his old friend, Ned.

Ned Morris led the way into the empty elevator and closed the door.

"It's really not such a great secret," he said. "Lots of the guests know it. The great Mortimer Mack, himself, said I could show it to you."

"Kind of him," was Wentworth's dry remark.

"Do you see this little panel at the back of the car?" continued Morris. "A spring holds it up." He pressed on it and pulled it down, revealing a button similar to the regular ones for the operation of the car. "Here we are on the top floor of Mortimer Mack's duplex apartment. You press on this button, and where do you think we go?"

"Don't know," said Wentworth, thinking of the apartment

two floors below where he had seen Dan Grogan. "Do you mind telling me where we do go?"

Ned Morris grinned broadly. "To the land of fair women and vanishing money," he said, pressing the button.

And the car shot upward.

CHAPTER 10
BLACKMAIL—AND MURDER!

JUST BEFORE the elevator reached the floor above Wentworth unexpectedly pressed the stop button and brought it to a halt. He placed a hand familiarly upon his companion's shoulder and spun him around.

"Ned," he asked, "as one old friend to another, what the devil are you doing at a show like this?"

Ned Morris grinned. "I might ask you the same question," he returned, "but, as a matter of fact, I'm working."

"Working?"

"Yes. You know I've been a reporter on *The Evening Star* ever since the family fortune went blooey in 1929."

"Surely you are not society reporting?"

Ned shook his head, his grin increasing. "There's a sprinkling of the old crowd here," he said, "but I wouldn't call this society." Suddenly he became serious. "Dick, there is something under the surface here, something rotten. Old Bannister, who owns my paper and a string of others, must be onto it. I'm reporting to him confidentially on what I can pick up. By the way, he is here himself tonight."

"Bannister? I haven't seen him."

"You probably will in a few minutes," returned Morris, pressing the secret button once more and shooting the car up again.

As the elevator came to rest at the next floor, soft music could be heard. It was low, throbbing music with an undertone of drums—drums which beat a rhythm that set the blood racing.

As the door of the elevator opened there was a burst of red, fiery light. A circular room, walled with mirrors, seemed to be on fire. It was illuminated entirely by means of twelve great braziers, from which tongues of red fire rose and fell flaringly to be multiplied a hundred-fold by the many surrounding mirrors. The low, savage beating of the drums became louder and shocked the ears, while the eyes were shocked by the glare of light.

And there was still more to shock the senses. Before two exits from this surprising room stood two women, chosen for their superb figures. One of the women was entirely encrusted with gold and the other with silver. And neither wore any clothing at all. Amid the flickering red fire they beckoned invitingly, each to her exit.

The drums, the red flare and the female forms were well calculated to shock and stimulate the new arrival.

"Hm!" ejaculated Wentworth, appraisingly. "Not bad, but I have seen better in Vienna."

Ned led the way toward the exit which was guarded by the woman in silver. Behind them the elevator door closed of itself and, itself a mirror, was lost amid the mirrors of the wall. Before them the silver woman threw up her arms in simulated joy because her exit had been chosen, while the woman in gold expressed anger at having been forsaken.

"Never mind, Goldie," called Ned jocularly to the angry woman, "we're only off the gold standard for a few minutes. Keep your coat of paint on."

As they passed through the silver-guarded entrance, the flaring fires died down behind them, leaving the room almost in gloom and the female figures shrouded within it.

It was evidently a little play enacted for each new arrival to whet the appetite for what was to come.

And what was to come spread itself before them as they parted heavy, silver portières and entered a great, oval room.

THE DRUMS were louder now, almost drowning the notes of barbaric instruments of African origin. Upon a floor of ebony black, which reflected those who stood upon it, the chorus of a popular hit was concluding an African dance. The skins of the women were dark, and their clothing consisted of very little more than the conventional strings of beads.

Around the oval wall, hung with thick, black velvet, were ranged broad, snow-white benches which were piled high with cushions of every conceivable color. Upon these pillowed benches reclined or sprawled, each to his or her alcoholic state of mind, the privileged guests who had been admitted to this super entertainment. Among them, treading carefully upon the smooth, black floor, waiters carried trays of champagne.

"Well, oh arbiter," asked Morris mockingly as they stood by the entrance for a moment, "are there enough unadorned women present to impress you?"

Richard Wentworth seemed more bored than surprised as he looked upon the scene. "I am of the opinion of Petronius," he remarked dryly, When he advised Caesar that ten thousand nude maidens make less impression than one."

As he spoke, the chorus ensemble ended, but the music of the drums did not cease. The continuous sound, with its tantalizingly missing beats, kept up its hammer-blows upon the brain. Here and there guests arose from the white benches and commenced to dance with their partners. Men, who had come alone, reached for the nearest "African" chorus girl and found her a willing partner in her string of beads.

Suddenly, through the throng upon the floor, Wentworth caught sight of the green, clinging dress of Cora. She was dancing with the same politician to whom he had abandoned her upon the floor below. He drew Ned's attention to the couple.

"That's Buckley, the politician," Ned commented. "He's a bit drunk. Might get a good story from him in his present condition. But he's nuts on Cora and no man could pry him loose from her."

"Suppose I pry her loose from him," suggested Wentworth indifferently.

"Well, you would be doing his wife a favor," returned Ned. "Hello! There's Jerry Stone butting in on them. Surely that poor little chap doesn't think he can split that pair!"

"And who is Jerry Stone!" asked Wentworth rather indifferently.

"He is a bit of a puzzle to me," admitted Ned. "He seems to be a cross between a favored employee and a poor relative of

Mortimer Mack—runs errands and does odd jobs in return for a glass of fizz water and a dance with the ladies."

Among the crowd of dancers Jerry Stone seemed to be having a hard time of it to attract Buckley's attention. He was no expert in cutting in on dancing couples, and his first tap on the politician's shoulder was quite unnoticed. The second was shaken off irritably, Buckley not even looking around to see who had annoyed him.

Wentworth, watching sharply, suddenly became aware of two interesting facts. The first was that Cora was leading a little in her dancing and quite evidently influencing her partner so that he would shortly come face to face with Jerry Stone. The second fact was that Mortimer Mack, himself, was standing behind a palm on the far side of the room and was watching Buckley keenly.

It seemed plain that Cora was working in co-operation with

THE WHEEL OF DEATH

The two men faced each other in silence

across the dead body of the politician.

Jerry, and that Mortimer Mack was watching the outcome of what was about to happen.

THEN IT was that Richard Wentworth also took a part, unexpectedly, in the little drama. Leaving his surprised friend suddenly, he threaded his way through the guests and dusky maidens of the chorus with that expert ease which can only come through long ballroom practice. He arrived at Cora's side just as Jerry once more laid his hand upon Buckley's shoulder, a hand in which there was a slip of paper.

It all happened so quickly as to be quite inexplicable to all save Wentworth. This time Jerry placed his hand, the hand with the paper, quite forcibly upon Buckley's shoulder.

The politician withdrew his right arm from around Cora's waist, probably with the intention of smiting the man who had interfered with him.

But at that moment Wentworth removed Cora's left arm from Buckley's shoulder and plucked the slip of paper from Jerry's hand.

Without a pause he spun Cora around with her back to Buckley and danced away with her into the throng before even she quite knew what was happening.

Behind them they left Buckley almost trembling with fury. Jerry Stone was looking on the floor for something he seemed to think he had dropped.

Most women like to be snatched away by a handsome man who knows how to wear evening clothes.

Cora was no exception.

"You devil!" she exclaimed. "But you'll get me into trouble."

"Then we'll mount our little sea horse and gallop away to Bermuda," Wentworth answered banteringly.

She drew her head back and looked at him hard. "Say, you aren't drunk any more," she said.

"Can't stay drunk when I'm away from you," he returned lightly.

She seemed puzzled and, while they danced, he worked the slip of paper in his left hand so that he could read it without her knowledge. It was a short, typewritten sentence:

Photostat copies of your letters to Cora will be mailed to your wife and to the press if the city does not vote a certain contract tomorrow.

Deftly Wentworth crumpled the little slip of paper into a ball and managed to hold it in the palm of his hand while he danced. Although no name appeared in the message, he had obtained definite indication that blackmail was being used to steal the city's money!

Cora, of course, was a professional manipulator of men, working, probably, upon salary and doing as she was told. Jerry Stone was a blundering tool, but did not quite seem to be either a fool or a knave. As for the master villain, who else could he be than Mortimer Mack?

The thought of Mack caused Wentworth to steer Cora toward the palm behind which he had seen the financier standing when Jerry Stone had been trying to deliver the anonymous, black-mailing note to Buckley. Mack was no longer there.

Slowly Wentworth circled the ballroom, talking glibly to

Cora while he searched among the dancers. Mortimer Mack was no longer in the room. Buckley and Jerry Stone seemed also to have disappeared, and Ned Morris was not to be seen.

Then Wentworth saw Nita. She was standing in the entrance, looking around the ballroom, and he knew instinctively that she was looking for him. She seemed, even at that distance, to be pale and a little unsteady. Wentworth hurriedly excused himself.

As he approached her, Nita saw him and came quickly to meet him, visibly pale and upset. "Oh, Dick!" she exclaimed in a low voice. "It is too terrible for words. They have just killed him."

"Killed him? Who has been killed?"

"That politician," she answered quickly. "The man who was dancing with the woman in green downstairs when we first came in!"

HE DREW her to one side out of the crowd, snatched a glass of wine for her from a passing servant, and listened to her story.

Just a few minutes ago she had gone to a ladies' dressing room near the great gambling salon which Wentworth had not yet seen. At the entrance to the dressing room she had seen the politician and Jerry Stone entering an adjacent room. The politician appeared to be very much upset about something, and Jerry Stone had seemed frightened.

In the dressing room Nita had been able to hear voices from the adjacent room into which the two men had entered. Alone for a few minutes, she had pressed her ear against the intervening wall and had heard the politician pleading with somebody not to do something.

"Dick, it was pitiful," Nita said. "That wretched man had some good in him. He was pleading for his wife and kids, pleading with all his heart. He said that he would do anything that he could, but that he couldn't do what they wanted—said he didn't have the power. When he talked about his wife and his children, they just laughed at him."

"Wait a minute," interrupted Wentworth. "Who laughed? Did Jerry Stone laugh?"

Nita shook her head and frowned, trying to remember. She did not think that Jerry Stone had laughed. She did not think that she had heard his voice through the wall at all. The laugh was in a deep, coarse, bellowing voice.

"His last word was his wife's name, Dick!" Nita shuddered. "Then came the shot and a groan and something falling, tumbling onto the floor."

"What happened when the shot was fired?" he asked quickly. "Didn't people come running?"

"No," she answered. "There was too much noise—laughter and drums! I am the only person who heard the shot."

"Can you find this murder room again?" he asked.

She nodded and led the way through a side door which led them out of the ballroom without passing through the reception room of red fire. A few steps along a passage brought them to the door of the ladies' dressing room, and Nita pointed to the door of the room next to it.

"In there," she whispered. "Oh, Dick! What are you going to do?"

"I am going to proceed with the taking apart of Mortimer Mack," was his quiet reply. "Is Ned Morris in the gambling salon, and can you find your way back there?"

"Yes, yes."

"Then go back there and tell Ned that I say he is not to leave you until I return."

There was nobody else in the passage, and as she walked slowly down its length, Wentworth stepped to the door which she had indicated, leaned his back against it. His hand, behind him, felt the knob and turned it. The door was locked. Quickly he took a bunch of curious keys from his pocket, selected one and inserted it in the lock. Quietly and expertly he turned the key. Then moving very swiftly, he faced the door, opened it and entered the room. Behind him he closed the door and locked it again.

The room was empty save for the silent form of Buckley upon the floor, where he lay with blood staining his shirt front. Book shelves lined the walls, and the furniture consisted of a flat desk, a chair and a steel safe, which appeared to be very efficient.

Wentworth knelt beside the still form and pulled open the shirt, bloodying his fingers a bit. As he did so, the man moved a little. Buckley was still alive, but the wound was bad and he was going fast. He was trying to speak, but his voice had almost failed him.

"Nellie!" he whispered. "Nellie mustn't know. Nellie and the kids mustn't—"

The whisper ceased—for Buckley was dead.

Behind him Wentworth, kneeling beside the dead man, heard a very slight click and the sound of a very soft footstep. He was certain that nobody had entered the door which he had locked behind him. There was only that one door, yet the room now held someone else in addition to himself—and the dead man.

He was unarmed and he had just penetrated a second secret of the iniquitous abode of Mortimer Mack—a ghastly secret, the discovery of which would probably bring vengeance dire and swift. And he knew that any sudden move on his part would bring that vengeance immediately.

CHAPTER 11
IN A TIGHT SPOT

I T WAS during such moments that Richard Wentworth depended upon his wit and his nerve. He rose casually from his stooping position beside the dead man, stepped leisurely over the body and selected a book from one of the shelves quite as if he did not know that some person stood behind him.

The book was a work on city government, a volume which had received considerable attention from the New York press because it dealt with the influence of politicians upon the government of the city. There had been talk of libel suits against the author and the publisher. But the politicians had so far failed to do anything about it.

"Interesting book?"

Wentworth recognized the soft voice of Mortimer Mack. But he read a sentence, at random, from the book before replying. "The elected officials of New York City," the author stated, "make no move and cast no vote except under the dictation of the politicians who arrange for their election or defeat at the polls."

Some of Buckley's blood, from one of Wentworth's fingers, smeared the page as he turned them, slowly, to face the man behind him.

"You may have the book if it interests you," said Mack suavely, as if they were indulging in an ordinary conversation.

The two men faced each other in silence for a few moments across the dead body of the politician who had forgotten his wife and family for the wiles of Cora. Outside the drums still throbbed and distant bursts of laughter could be faintly heard.

But if Mortimer Mack could be suave and casual, so also could Richard Wentworth. He opened the book again where his bloody fingers had kept the place and read aloud. "The politicians sway the voting of the ignorant masses and indirectly rule the city despotically. It only remains for an arch rogue to arise who will coerce the politicians and reduce the city to a state of absolute slavery."

Unconcernedly Wentworth closed the book and returned it to its place on the shelf. "It would seem as though the arch rogue had arisen!" he said calmly.

Mortimer Mack smiled and nodded his head as if he were

too polite to contradict a guest. Casually he took an automatic pistol from his pocket.

Swiftly Wentworth took a pace toward him, ready to strike it from his hand or wrench it from him, if he should attempt to shoot. An agile man can do this nine times out of ten, if he is close enough and if he is trained to self-defense.

Mortimer Mack, however, did not raise the pistol threateningly. On the contrary, he kept it pointed toward the floor while he carefully wiped the grip and barrel with his handkerchief, evidently with the intention of removing all finger prints. Then, holding it with the handkerchief, he placed it upon the floor not far from one of the dead man's hands.

"It was with this pistol that Buckley was killed," he said. "The bullet passed through him and is lodged among the books behind you, Mr. Wentworth. The police can prove that this is the pistol which was used by measuring the lands and grooves of the rifling and comparing them with the markings on the bullet."

"I scarcely need such elementary instructions," remarked Wentworth lightly.

"There is more." Mortimer Mack pursed his lips and allowed his eyebrows to remain elevated for a moment in an expression of grotesque sternness. "A man was killed at Grogan's Restaurant by a bullet which bears the same markings that are upon the bullet in the books behind you. The pistol, of course, is numbered, and a confidential search at Police Headquarters has revealed to us the fact that it belongs to you, Mr. Wentworth."

"Stolen," laconically commented Wentworth without any trace of embarrassment.

"Not very convincing," retorted Mack acidly, "since we have plenty of witnesses that you were here tonight. In addition, the girl, Molly Dennis, can be forced to give evidence that you were in Grogan's Restaurant when the killings occurred at that place. The evidence against you is damning—my dear Mr. Spider!"

RICHARD WENTWORTH laughed. The little man may have thought that he was acting and that the laugh was mere bravado. But the laugh was genuine and came from sheer joy at the news that little Molly was still alive. The uncertainty of her fate had worried Wentworth, since he blamed himself for what might have happened to her.

Yet Wentworth's position was precarious in the extreme. It might seem a simple thing for him to pick up his pistol and take his departure from the room, leaving Mortimer Mack either dead or alive as he wished. Wentworth, however, knew that his opponent was no fool and was certain that he must have taken precautions. Had he not entered the room while the door remained closed? Certainly there must be some secret entrance to the room, probably through the bookcase, and, with equal probability, other eyes were watching the scene through some small aperture, perhaps over the sights of a pistol.

Mack seemed to sense Wentworth's thoughts. "I am not fool enough to put myself in your power," he said, "so please exercise discretion." He paused and looked down at the still form upon the floor. "I could stretch you lifeless beside your dead friend at any moment that I chose!"

"Then why do you wait?" asked Wentworth indifferently.

Mortimer Mack merely shrugged his shoulders.

"Shall I tell *you?*" continued Wentworth, smiling. "It is because you do not know how much I have discovered and you think that I, also, may have taken precautions." He paused and looked down at the dead man. "If I were dead, you might not be able to avoid my precautions. But while I am alive you hope to coerce me."

Suddenly Mortimer Mack turned toward the door in a listening attitude. Wentworth also stood very still, listening. Something strange had happened. The subdued throbbing of the barbaric drums had ceased. There was no more music, but there was the sound of people scurrying along the passage outside the door. Something unusual and unexpected had happened.

The little man moved nervously toward the door, puzzled and obviously disturbed.

"Just one of *my* precautions," taunted Wentworth, although he had no knowledge of what was happening.

A woman screamed and Mortimer Mack fumbled in his pocket for the key to the door.

Wentworth took a step nearer to the pistol which lay upon the floor. This might be his only opportunity to recover the weapon which he had lost. He placed his foot in front of the pistol and waited.

Another woman screamed, and somebody shouted an alarming word: "Police!"

Trembling with anger and excitement, Mortimer Mack

inserted the key in the lock and opened the door slightly. As he did so, Wentworth sprang forward kicking the pistol to the door in his rush.

At the door he literally butted Mack out into the hall and, at the same time, scooped the pistol from the floor as he followed him out of the room.

People are always upset by the sudden presence of the police. Their invasion of a place of entertainment, no matter how innocent that place may be, is alarming. And in Mortimer Mack's extraordinary establishment there was much hurrying about by excited, frightened people. Dusky maidens of the chorus scampered barefooted, thinking the house was pinched. Guests, more dignified, considered that the intrusion of the police was an outrage.

Mack himself was almost purple with suppressed fury as he stood in the passage with Wentworth, his back to the door of the room they had just left.

"Damn you!" he exclaimed, and his voice was not at all suave. It was evident that he believed Wentworth had in some way managed to summon the law.

The police came straight and fast, three uniformed men and a plainclothesman. Without any hesitation they entered the passage and advanced toward the door before which stood Wentworth and Mack.

Behind them, half running, and dragging Ned Morris by the hand, came Nita. She was very pale, and her eyes strained to see Wentworth over the bobbing shoulders of the policemen ahead of her.

Mortimer Mack, summoning his dignity, stepped forward to meet the legal intruders. He expressed surprise and demanded a search warrant, but they brushed him aside.

"We got a phone call that Buckley's been bumped off," said the detective, placing his hand on the knob of the door. "This is the room—second on the left of the passage."

He flung open the door and stepped inside. Behind him Wentworth glanced through the open doorway. It was a quiet room, lined with book shelves and containing a very fine steel safe and a flat-topped desk. But there was no corpse or trace of any corpse!

"Geez!" exclaimed the detective. "I wonder if that was a phony call we got. The young fellow's voice was so scared that I thought it must be on the level!"

CHAPTER 12
POLICE THREAT

ORDER BEGAN to manifest itself amid the excitement. The police stood in a little knot, talking with Mortimer Mack, who was meeting their arguments with a mixture of ridicule and indignation. From the ends of the passage, and at the entrance to the ballroom, guests and dusky chorus girls crowded and peered. But voices were now reduced to normal, and there was beginning to be heard little ripples of laughter. It was thought that some absurd mistake had been made by the police and that nothing of an alarming nature had happened.

Some began to drift back to the ballroom. Music commenced

again. The night was still young at Mortimer Mack's weekly entertainment.

Nita stood with Wentworth and Ned Morris not far from the group of policemen who talked with Mortimer Mack. They could just hear their conversation, especially the words of the policemen.

"Geez!" exclaimed the detective again. "Of course I could recognize the voice. It was like a kid's voice, and he seemed scared to death. That's why I was so sure that something was wrong. He was too scared to be acting."

Ned nudged his friend, Wentworth. "Corking inside page story," he said. "Even the rumor of Buckley's murder is news in New York."

"And a corking front page story if the rumor is true," commented Wentworth dryly.

Ned Morris looked at his friend sharply and shrewdly. He was a good newspaper man, and he knew that Wentworth was not given to foolish imaginings.

"Surely," he said in surprise after a pause, "you do not think that this story is true?"

Indifferently, his face quite without expression, Wentworth opened his right hand, exposing his bloody fingers for Morris to see. "Some of Buckley's last blood," he said, watching the effect upon his slightly younger friend, while Nita raised her handkerchief and looked away, struggling to control her emotions.

"Good God, man!" exclaimed Ned in amazement. Then as

his mind grasped the significance of what he had seen: "Dick, don't tell me that you did it!"

"Would I show you these fingers if I had done it?" Wentworth asked, smiling.

"You might!" Ned returned. "There is nothing on earth that you might not take it into your head to do."

"Except hurt somebody who shouldn't be hurt," Nita interrupted unexpectedly.

Ned nodded, agreeing with that statement, but still looking at Wentworth in amazement. "Why aren't you telling this to the police?" he asked. "Why are you telling me?"

"I am not telling the police," returned Wentworth, "because the thing is too hideous and too gigantic to be broken into yet. Premature disclosure would ruin things."

"Are you just telling me out of friendship?"

"No." Wentworth shook his head decisively. "I may be bumped off sometime in the next few hours, possibly even while I stand here talking to you. If so, I want you to use the information I am giving you. Buckley was shot to death about half an hour ago in the little room over there. I do not know who shot him. The bullet passed through his body and lodged among some book shelves. Some of his blood from my fingers is smeared upon page two hundred and five of a book entitled "City Government," which is upon the fourth shelf from the bottom. Analysis of the blood upon that page will show that the corpuscles are in the same proportion to the corpuscles in the blood of Buckley—if his body is ever found. As for me, Nita is a witness that I did not do it."

"And I suppose that this is in strict confidence until the dire event of your popping off?" asked Ned with a grin, under the urge of his newspaper complex for treating tragedy lightly.

"Absolute confidence," agreed Wentworth.

"Ssh!" interrupted Nita before anything else could be said. She was looking toward Mortimer Mack and the policemen, who still stood in front of the room in which a murder was rumored to have been committed.

Mortimer Mack was smiling holding up his hands. "Just to be thorough," he stated good naturedly, "I wish one of you would search me to see if I have the rumored pistol with which the rumored murder was rumored to have been committed. I was discussing politics with my friend, Mr. Richard Wentworth, just a few minutes ago in the very room where the murder was said to have happened. I am sure that Mr. Wentworth would like to be searched also."

The attack upon Richard Wentworth had come even while he stood talking to Ned Morris, as he had suggested. WENTWORTH REALIZED that Mortimer Mack knew that he had recovered his pistol in the confusion just before the police reached the door. If the police found that weapon upon his person it would be a simple matter for somebody, probably anonymously, to give the information that it was the pistol which had fired one of the bullets in the two killings at Grogan's Restaurant. Comparison of the lands and grooves with the bullet markings, together with evidence brought from Molly Dennis under cross examination, would certainly damn him in the eyes of the law.

It was another one of those tight situations which Wentworth often sought for the thrill of the thing, and which sometimes came to him without any seeking by reason of the adventurous life which he led.

In full evening clothes there is only one place where so heavy and bulky an article as a pistol can be carried or concealed. This is in the pocket of the coat tails. But even in that pocket the weight of a pistol will somewhat disrupt the hang of the coat.

Now Wentworth felt the weight of his recovered pistol where it pulled down on one of the tails of his coat, and knew that it threatened his life.

The detective, rather hesitatingly, was making a perfunctory search of Mortimer Mack, patting him here and there and feeling his coat tails. Of course the net result of the search was nil.

Mortimer Mack bobbed his eyebrows and pursed his lips in his characteristic manner. He smiled toward Wentworth. "And now," he said, "my friend, Mr. Richard Wentworth, would surely like to be relieved of all odium in connection with rumored murder."

The detective, who was now sure that he had been the victim of a hoax, came slowly toward Wentworth, where he stood between Nita and Ned Morris. "I scarcely think it is necessary," he said.

"Oh, but I insist!" exclaimed Mortimer Mack, smiling. "I cannot allow a guest to leave here with the slightest suspicion of any stigma attached to him."

Wentworth laughed and, standing close between Nita and

Ned, placed an arm suddenly upon the shoulder of each. His quick movement swung the heavy weight in his tail pocket forcibly against Nita's thigh. It was his only chance. Would she understand—and could she do anything?

THE DETECTIVE came on. Nita's hand, hanging by her side, slipped into the tail pocket behind Wentworth's back. It came out, bringing the pistol with it. She pressed the weapon close to her where it was shielded from view by Wentworth's body.

But the weapon was too big for her to conceal upon her person. What could she do with it when Wentworth moved away to be searched?

And Wentworth did move away, taking a step or two to meet the detective. He had felt the weight vanish from the tail of his coat and he moved so that his body shielded Nita from the eyes of the man who was about to search him.

During the second perfunctory search by the detective, Wentworth looked into the eyes of Mortimer Mack. Both sets of eyes seemed to be smiling. But Wentworth felt something venomous and ugly behind Mack's eyes, especially as the search again ended in failure. He saw the eyes of a man who could smile while he hated—who could probably kill while he laughed.

The police withdrew. The drums sounded again and the spectacular entertainment continued.

Ned Morris caught Wentworth by the arm as he was about to dance away with Nita toward the ballroom.

"Look here, old man," Ned half whispered, "Nita slipped

something into my tail pocket. I don't know what it is, and I don't *want* to know what it is."

"You're a rotten reporter if there's something you don't want to know," remarked Wentworth jocularly.

"It's only because we grew up together that I'm acting this way, Dick."

"I know, old man," was Wentworth's quiet reply. "By the way, I want you to do me a favor."

From his vest pocket Wentworth took a small tablet with a gold pencil attached. For a few moments he scribbled on the top sheet before tearing it off and handing it to Ned, who could not help looking at the unfolded sheet.

"Holy smoke!" Ned exclaimed. "It looks like the scratchings of a hen."

"Hindustani characters," explained Wentworth. "Take it over to my place, like a good chap, and give it to my man, Ram Singh. I think you know him. He will give you something to bring back to me. Mind doing it?"

"Certainly not! I'll go at once, but what about this damned thing in my pocket?"

"Oh, I told Ram Singh to pick that out of your pocket when you weren't looking."

Without waiting for any reply, so well did he know and trust his friend, Wentworth placed his arm around Nita and swept her away, into and around the ballroom.

From one end of the ballroom to the other they danced, while Wentworth searched rapidly among the guests and chorus girls who had again abandoned themselves to dancing, drinking and laughter without any further thoughts of murders, rumored or otherwise. But among the dancers, and upon the white, pillow-covered benches, there were no persons whom he sought. Mortimer Mack was not present, and there was no trace of Cora nor of Jerry Stone. Of course Dan Grogan was not to be seen, and poor old Buckley would never dance again.

"And now for the halls, the passages and the weird entrance with the red fires by the elevator," said Wentworth as they came again to the end of the ballroom. "I am studying the layout of this place."

"And there's the gambling salon," added Nita. "You haven't seen that yet."

But Wentworth shook his head. He didn't want to see that until he had fixed the rest of the floor thoroughly in his mind and had arrived at a certain conclusion which was just beginning to dawn upon him. Through the passages and halls they sauntered, arm in arm, apparently talking innocently while he considered the arrangement of the various walls and even measured distances by counting his steps as he walked. It was a very large floor, occupying one entire wing of the huge apartment house, and undoubtedly had been especially designed for the man who had leased or bought it.

IT WAS at last among the twelve red fires, which leaped from the twelve great braziers, that Wentworth came to a halt with Nita upon his arm. The golden lady and the silver lady had risen to attention upon their entrance, ready to express their sorrow upon the departure of two guests.

But Wentworth did not press the button for the elevator,

and the metal-coated, female adornments stood at attention, waiting to see what the two guests, so distinguished in appearance, would decide to do. Surrounded by the many mirrors they stood among hundreds of red fires, hundreds of gold and silver female forms, reflected and otherwise.

"*Cherie,*" said Wentworth to Nita, breaking into rapid French while he watched the faces of the two attendants until he was confident that they did not understand that language, "there is something very surprising in the arrangement of this place." He tapped one of the mirrors between two of the big braziers. "Do you know what lies on the other side of that mirror?"

She shook her head.

"On the other side of that," he stated, "is the ladies' dressing room, the room from which you heard the fatal shot fired."

"Oh!" she exclaimed. "I did not realize that the passage led back in this direction."

"And what is more important," he continued, "the little study, in which the killing was done, lies to the left of the dressing room as you know. Such being the case, it becomes necessary for one of the study walls to be adjacent to the elevator shaft!"

"Which means?" she asked, looking puzzled.

He pointed at the red flame, leaping from one of the braziers near the elevator, as if he were commenting upon its beauty. "It means," he said, "that there is a secret entrance from the murder room to the elevator.

"Oh!" exclaimed Nita. "There is something diabolically clever about this place."

As she finished speaking the door of the elevator opened

and Jerry Stone emerged, pale and looking very scared. He hurried across the room without looking at them and passed quickly through the entrance to the gambling salon, the entrance presided over by the woman who was covered with the plastic gold.

Neither of the women attendants paid any attention to him, and it would seem that he was an habitué of the place who escaped the ceremonies which were accorded to guests.

Wentworth tightened his grip upon Nita's arm. "There goes a young fool to his death," he said swiftly and quietly in the French language.

"But why, Dick?" asked Nita in horror. "Why?"

"Because," returned Wentworth, "Jerry Stone is the man who informed the police about the murder of Buckley. At first Mortimer Mack thought that I had done it—but now he must know. Jerry Stone will be dead very soon, unless—"

"Unless what, Dick?"

"Come on!" he answered. "It is just possible that I can save him—for Molly. Let's go!"

Arm in arm they passed out of the room of glaring fires into the gambling salon. The golden curtain parted for their passage. The golden woman writhed her supple body in an ecstasy of simulated joy because her entrance had been selected.

Behind them the red fires died down until the arrival of other guests....

CHAPTER 13
NITA DISAPPEARS

T HEY CAME into a large room which was brilliantly lighted. The walls were richly hung with gold, but not otherwise ornamented. Down the center of the room was an unusually large roulette table, a full thirty feet long, and seated around it were as many guests, men and women, as could find room. Behind the players other guests stood, watching the game and waiting a chance to join in.

"Rein ne va plus!"

The croupier's voice was authoritative and professional, as he announced in French that no more stakes would be accepted. The little ball was coming to rest, and conversation died down as the players waited to learn if they had won or lost.

"Treize, rouge, impair, manque," called the croupier, as the ball came to rest and the players knew that they had won if they had staked upon number thirteen, upon red numbers, upon odd numbers or upon numbers from one to eighteen inclusive.

There were four croupiers who shot their little rakes expertly over the green cloth to gather in the stakes of those who had lost, while some exclamations of pleasure or of disappointment escaped from the players according to their fortune.

"By Jove!" exclaimed Wentworth to Nita as they halted a little distance from the table. "It sounds like a professional game. Those croupiers are certainly imported from France."

"Do you suppose the game is on the level?" asked Nita in a whisper.

"Of course it's on the level," returned Wentworth. "In the long run the bank always wins. Roulette doesn't need to be crooked."

"But how can he get away with such open gambling week after week in New York City?" Nita asked.

"Political influence, my dear, will do anything in New York City," was the dry response.

"But it seems absurd that so wealthy and important a business man as Mortimer Mack should descend to professional gambling," she persisted.

Wentworth smiled. "Nita," he said, "I do not think that Mortimer Mack is giving New York such excellent roulette for the purpose of making money. Suppose that a politician should lose more than he could afford. Suppose that he gave an I.O.U. that he could not meet, or wrote a check without sufficient funds in the bank. Gambling has placed many a man in another man's power."

"Look!" exclaimed Nita. "There is Jerry Stone standing beside Mortimer Mack on the other side of the table behind the two croupiers."

"Yes, I have been watching them," said Wentworth. "And do you see that elderly man seated before the *manqué* space at Mack's right? That is old David Bannister, owner of a string of newspapers and, incidentally, the employer of Ned Morris. He is a power in the state."

"I certainly am surprised to see such a man as that at a roulette table in defiance of the law," said Nita.

"Has it occurred to you," asked Wentworth, "that David Bannister may be conducting an investigation of his own?"

Suddenly Nita nudged her companion. "There goes Jerry Stone," she said. "Mortimer Mack just spoke to him, and he's going toward the passage which leads to that terrible room where they ended poor Buckley."

Wentworth nodded, adding: "He'll never come back alive." NITA TURNED pale. "Oh, Dick!" she exclaimed. "Can't you do something before it's too late?"

"If only Ned Morris had come back with what I sent him for!" complained Wentworth in a low voice.

But he left her and went swiftly across the room toward the exit which young Stone was approaching. He had not really needed Nita's urging, but had simply been waiting for the right moment to start into action.

They met, the unsophisticated youngster in the poorly fitting dinner jacket and the more experienced man, exactly at the exit. They seemed to meet by accident—very much by accident since Wentworth bumped rather violently into young Stone.

Polished and fluent expressions of apology flowed from Wentworth. He seized the younger man by the arm and again remembered him as the man he had met at Monte Carlo. Or was it Nice? Now that they had met again, it didn't matter. They would have a drink together and then they would risk a little money at roulette just as they had done at Monte Carlo. Or was it Marseilles?

Before Jerry Stone quite knew what was happening to him, he was dragged half way back into the room. But Jerry was one of those men who are a trifle weak from lack of worldly experience. He became flustered and, when such a man becomes flustered, he sometimes becomes stubborn. Jerry became stubborn in an endeavor to offset his lack of composure. He had started out to do something and he insisted upon doing it, after which he was willing enough to have a drink but could not afford to play roulette.

Wentworth, still holding Jerry with friendly firmness by the arm, glimpsed Mortimer Mack approaching them. Nita, too, was advancing toward them, to be of assistance if that were possible. A hush seemed to have fallen upon the room. The guests seemed to be waiting for something.

Then Wentworth saw that Mack held a check in his hand.

"Mr. Wentworth," said the little man, extending the check, "you are a new guest at our roulette table, and I should be happy if you would do us a little favor."

Mortimer Mack's manner was very friendly, and it was difficult to believe that he had so recently confronted Wentworth over the body of a murdered man. His face was twitching a little, but there was a smile upon it.

"Yes?" questioned Wentworth easily. "What may I do for you?"

"My croupiers report to me that the bank has a profit of five thousand dollars," explained Mack. "All our profits are given to charity and, each night, I ask a different guest to name the charity to which the profits shall he paid. Tonight, Mr. Wentworth, I should be happy if you would name the charity so that I may write it upon this check and give it to you to deliver."

"The Salvation Army is a good charity," answered Wentworth quickly.

"Excellent!" exclaimed Mack. He fumbled in his pocket as if for a pen with which to write the name upon the check. "Ah, Mr. Stone, would you mind stepping to my study and bringing me a pen? You will find one upon the desk, I think."

"And Jerry, old man," said Wentworth quickly, "hurry back for that drink, or I'll send the whole police force of New York City after you!"

Wentworth had released his grip on Jerry Stone's arm and was looking straight into Mortimer Mack's eyes as he spoke of the New York police force. Although the words were lightly spoken, they were really a very dire threat to Mortimer Mack.

"Do you really think the New York police force would be of much assistance, Mr. Wentworth?" asked Mortimer Mack with equal lightness. "They are so busy looking for the Spider, that strange New York killer, you know."

Mack's words were a return threat to Wentworth. Between the two men there was now war which could only end in the death of one of them.

IT WAS at that moment that a voice sounded behind Wentworth, and turning he beheld David Bannister, the great newspaper publisher, holding out a pen to Mortimer Mack. It seemed incredible that so powerful and important a man as Bannister should act the handmaid to Mortimer Mack, or to any man. Yet he had given up his seat at the roulette table and crossed the floor to extend his pen rather than allow Mack to wait a few minutes for Jerry Stone to return.

Bannister did not look like a man who would allow himself to be caught by the wiles of a woman such as Cora. His clear eyes and steady hand as he held the pen gave no indication of the dope victim, and he was worth so many millions that it would appear impossible for him to have been ruined by gambling.

Yet Mortimer Mack took the pen from him without any evidence of surprise. He filled in the blank on the check and handed it to Wentworth, who tucked it carelessly in a vest pocket, then turned to look for Nita.

But Nita was not there!

Instantly Wentworth knew what had happened. Nita had followed Jerry Stone, thinking that she might in some way save him when Wentworth seemed to be delayed. The question filled his mind: Had she entered the room in which the murder occurred? He hoped that she had not done so, that she had induced Jerry to stay away from it. But he knew that it was in her character to be daring.

When he turned again, Mortimer Mack was still smiling. But the smile now seemed to have additional meaning—to have taken on a tinge of triumph.

"Rien ne va plus," called the croupier.

The words, "Nothing more goes," seemed to have a portentous meaning, as though a direful end had come. The clicking of the little ball died away and, in the brilliantly lighted room, voices hushed while the players waited for the announcement.

"Well, here are your bally cigars."

Wentworth turned quickly to receive a leather case from his

friend, Ned Morris, who had just arrived. It was a trifle longer than is used for perfectos and perhaps a little thicker, but it dropped easily into the tail pocket of Wentworth's coat.

Then, as David Bannister and Mortimer Mack, shoulder to shoulder very confidentially, walked slowly back to the roulette table, Wentworth felt another tug upon one of the tails of his coat. Ned, standing very close to him, had dropped something else into the same pocket, something quite heavy.

"That surprising Indian servant of yours," explained Ned in a low voice, "insisted upon my bringing you a funny looking piece of artillery. He said, 'Him no want, you bring back.' Seemed to think I was a nice messenger boy."

"Thanks, old man," returned Wentworth warmly if briefly. "Do as much for you some time."

In another moment he had turned upon his heel and was walking swiftly toward the exit to the passage which led to the study where Mortimer Mack kept his flat-topped desk and steel safe. There was more lightness in his heart. The "funny looking piece of artillery" was, as he knew, his powerful air pistol which had been made for him by one of the cleverest of mechanicians, a man he had once saved from ruin.

There were few things that Wentworth would not attempt with that pistol in his pocket, with his bunch of curious keys and with the contents of the leather folder which so much resembled a large cigar case.

IN THE long passage, which led past Mortimer Mack's study, he met no one. The door of the study was open, and the room appeared to be empty. He hurried on and turned into the side entrance to the ballroom, where heavy curtains hung.

For a moment he glanced into the ballroom. It was much the same scene as before except that some guests had gone home and those who remained were not quite so sober. Drawing the curtains partly aside, he looked back at the study door. It was still open, and he glanced beyond it back along the passage toward the side entrance of the gambling salon. He expected to be followed, and he was waiting to see by whom.

He had not long to wait. He was expecting Mortimer Mack, and he received a surprise. Out from the entrance of the gambling salon came Nita. She was walking quickly but, as he watched, she stopped at the open door of the study and looked in. Wentworth, fearful that she might enter that dangerous room, was on the point of stepping out into the passage to meet her, when a long arm shot out and Nita was gone, dragged roughly into the room.

Wentworth sprang into the passage, almost tearing down one of the curtains in his rush. It was only a matter of seconds before he was at the door of the study with his hand on the knob. But the door was locked. It was a stout door, and he knew that he could tease the lock open with one of his strange keys before he could break it down.

Rapidly he selected a key, fitted it into the lock and gently nursed it this way and that until the lock moved. In less than half a minute from the time Nita had disappeared, he flung open the door and leaped into the room, ready to kill any man who resisted him.

But the study, with its shelves of books, its flat-topped desk and its big steel safe, was quite empty.... There was no sign of Nita Van Sloan within the room!

CHAPTER 14
AGAIN THE SEAL

IT WAS only for a few seconds that Richard Wentworth stood inactive within that quiet, harmless-appearing study. But in that brief flash of time his mind assembled the known facts, drew deductions therefrom and arrived at a conclusion as to the best course of action.

Without doubt there was some secret exit from Mortimer Mack's study—and that exit almost certainly opened into the automatic elevator. Probably some section of the bookcase was hinged secretly to swing out.

To find that contrivance, however, would take time even for a man like Richard Wentworth. But he *could* find the elevator, or at least the elevator shaft, without any delay. And he could smash open the elevator door, in the fantastic room of the twelve red fires—perhaps in time to intercept the slow-moving elevator as it bore Nita downward to the unknown apartment below Mortimer Mack's gorgeous duplex establishment.

Only a few seconds had elapsed since Nita had been dragged into the study, and he felt certain that he could reach the elevator shaft before the creeping car could have gone by.

Out into the passageway Wentworth darted and through the side entrance into the ballroom. He skirted the big dancing floor so rapidly that he brought exclamations of disapproval from some of the guests with whom he collided.

But Wentworth's rush came to a sudden stop as he entered the reception room where the red fires blazed fitfully and the startling female attendants postured. The elevator door was open and two guests, a man and a woman, were entering, evidently with the intention of going home.

Certainly there had been no time for the elevator to descend and rise again since Nita had been captured. It would seem as though she must be separated from Wentworth only by the mirror-covered wall, her captor waiting, no doubt, to secure the service of the elevator when it was not being used by any of the guests.

Such being the case, Wentworth decided to take possession of the elevator at once and to maintain possession until he had mastered all its secrets. He pushed rapidly into the elevator behind the two guests who were ahead of him.

The door closed, and the car began to descend as Wentworth pressed the first button of the control. His two companions, waiting for the elevator to reach the first floor of the duplex establishment, whispered a few words about the weather while they thought of other things. Wentworth only thought about getting rid of both of them, so that he could use the elevator for his own purposes.

The car came to a stop, and the door opened. Naturally Wentworth stood back to allow the lady and her escort to pass out. Immediately that they had done so, he quickly closed the door again and remained within the car. He pressed neither of

"Damn you!" he exclaimed furiously. "Drop that gun or I'll slit her throat!"

the visible buttons which controlled the car, nor did he move the secret panel to press the button which would return the car once more to the level of the gambling salon. Somewhere he believed, behind the mirrors of the entrance room on that floor, there must be a secret entrance to the elevator. Another side of the car must be cleverly contrived to open upon a hidden exit from the study.

He felt certain that there must be a concealed master control of the elevator, by means of which it could be secretly operated in defiance of any calls which might be made upon it by the pressing of the usual, exposed buttons. He believed that such a call would presently be made upon it, for the purpose of carrying Nita three stories down to the apartment where he had stumbled upon Grogan and Cora.

He waited while one of his hands felt the deadly air pistol in the tail pocket of his coat. This time he would go into action in all probability, and it would be his life or another's.

SUDDENLY THE car gave a lurch and commenced to ascend. Somebody had summoned it from above. It might be a guest, or it might be one of the underworld who were helping Mortimer Mack in his amazing attempt to subjugate the great city of New York. If it were a guest, Wentworth could do little more than descend again and wait for another call upon the car. If, however, the front door of the elevator did not open, and if a false side of it fell away to expose the study entrance! Wentworth felt the weapon in his pocket and waited.

The car had scarcely ascended one story when Wentworth, his mind always active, realized that there might be some cunning way by means of which his enemies could see into the car and become aware of his presence before entering it. Above his head there was a single electric light bulb. He was tall enough to reach it easily, and he unscrewed it until the connection was broken. The elevator was plunged into complete darkness.

The car continued to ascend slowly, as is the nature of automatic elevators, while Wentworth kept his hand upon the electric light bulb. If the usual front door opened, he would give the bulb a twist, thus illuminating the car for any guests who might enter. If, however, the front door did *not* open, and if another side of the elevator moved, then there might be light or no light, life or no life. Wentworth was grimly determined.

In due course the elevator came to a stop after an interval which was sufficient to allow it to reach the floor of the gambling salon. Very faintly Wentworth could hear the barbaric music from the ballroom and, still more faintly, he heard voices, probably the voices of guests. Nothing happened. For a moment he stood perfectly motionless, his hand upon the cooling bulb above his head.

Then, abruptly, there was a slight click. In the dark he could see nothing—but a side of the elevator *touched* him. It was moving inward, swinging upon hinges so well oiled that there was no sound. As the moving partition touched him, Wentworth crouched swiftly in a far corner of the elevator. His deadly pistol was now out of his pocket and ready for instant action.

In the darkness Wentworth heard a heavy step and felt its impact upon the floor of the elevator. There was a smothered, feminine protest, and he recognized Nita's voice. Still he waited, crouching low. He heard a muttered comment in a man's angry, unpleasant voice.

Above his head then he heard the slight sound of the electric light bulb being touched, and knew that the man had found it loose and was screwing it tight again. In one more second he would be in conflict.

Blindingly, after the intense darkness, the elevator became illuminated as the bulb once more made contact. Above him Wentworth saw a man who held Nita firmly by one arm as he gave the bulb a last tightening turn. Nita, gagged, but otherwise free except for the man's restraining arm, had her back to Wentworth and stood between him and her captor.

Over her shoulder the man, evidently a character of the underworld, looked straight down at Wentworth who still crouched, pistol in hand, in the corner.

The man was startled, but he was quick and he was vicious. His hand dropped from the electric light bulb like a flash and rose instantly from a breast pocket with a knife, an ugly weapon with a shining, queerly pointed blade. The point of that knife hovered half an inch from Nita's throat!

Nita, startled, tried still harder to draw away from the man, but his powerful arm pressed her tightly against him. Shielded by her, the man kept his head as much as possible behind her head and watched Wentworth warily with only one eye.

"Damn you!" he exclaimed furiously. "Drop that gun, or I'll slit her throat!"

IT WAS the most difficult shot that Wentworth had ever been called upon to make. The target was that single, evil eye.

If he missed it on one side, the man would probably plunge his knife into Nita's throat. If he missed it on the other side, he would probably send his bullet through Nita's head.

Nita, although she could not see, seemed to grasp the situation at once. With her free hand she managed to tug the gag partly away from her mouth.

"Shoot, Dick!" she exclaimed. "You can do it."

It was like her heroic self to urge him, and it was like her to know that it could only be he who had come to her rescue. Probably he would have fired if she had not spoken. As it was, he pressed the trigger on the sound of her last word, and—he did not miss.

The dangerous shot went straight to the target, and the peering eye went out, never to see again. Nor would its mate ever again behold anything more in this world. The man who hid behind a woman and pressed a knife against her throat was dead.

Even as the man slumped upon the floor of the elevator, and his knife clattered beside him, Wentworth caught Nita and spun her around, pressing her close to him. He removed the gag and pressed her lips where it had been.

"My dear!" he exclaimed. "Can you ever forgive me for letting this happen to you?"

Her answer was silence and willingness to remain in his arms. There is no better answer that a man may have from a woman.

But their respite from action was brief.

"Don't look down," he said as he guided her around the dead man on the floor of the elevator and into what appeared to be

125

a large steel box which had been exposed by the opening of the elevator's false side. And he realized then that they stood within the steel safe in the study! It was not a safe after all, but only a masked entrance to the elevator!

She stood behind him while he went to work. First there was the door of the steel box, which so resembled a safe when viewed from the study, to be examined. It took but a glance to show that it could be opened very simply by throwing over a bolt on the inside, although, no doubt, it required the use of the combination to open it from the study side.

Next there was the matter of the secret control of the elevator, and this he found exposed upon the outside of the false side which had opened and which still remained open. Here there was another control box, a master control box. Upon it were two buttons, one of which would send the car to the secret apartment three stories below. This button was already pushed in and the car would, no doubt, begin its descent upon the closing of the false door.

Lastly there was the matter of the dead man in the elevator. Who he was, Wentworth did not know, but he felt quite confident that he was connected with Mortimer Mack and with Dan Grogan in their gigantic plot to entrap New York City. Leaving Nita in the steel box, Wentworth bent over the dead man. He found nothing of interest in the pockets, but drew a heavy pistol from the dead man's hip pocket—where it had been too low for him to seize quickly enough when unexpectedly confronted by Wentworth in the elevator.

RELUCTANTLY, BUT without hesitation, Wentworth

pocketed the heavy pistol and placed his own air pistol in the dead man's hand, carefully wiping it free from all finger prints. The air pistol, confidentially made for him by his old friend, was not registered with the police and could not be traced to him. But it might prove awkward if found upon his person while he was still in the vicinity of a man who had died from one of its bullets.

There was one more thing, a reckless thing perhaps, but one that fitted into the nature of the man who ran so many risks and who witted himself against such terrific odds. From the lithe pocket of his tight-fitting white vest he took a cigarette lighter. It was not the same lighter that he had used when he had placed the seal of the Spider upon the foreheads of the gunmen at Grogan's Restaurant, though in outward appearance it was quite similar.

As he broke the varnished junction and extracted the notorious seal, which was contained in the secret cavity, he wondered if he would ever have to use the subtle invention which his old friend, the professor, wrought into it. He little knew how soon that test would come.

Deftly and with the laboratory precision of a scientist, he stamped the vermilion outline of the little spider upon the cheek of the dead man, just under the place which had once been an eye. The door of the elevator rattled as he did so. Some guest was becoming impatient for the arrival of the car, but the secret, master control held the front door locked until the false side had been closed and the car sent upon its special bidding, three stories below.

All this had required but a few seconds, so quickly and with such assurance did Wentworth work. Nita, in the great steel box, saw Wentworth return the cigarette lighter to his pocket as he joined her.

She knew the secret of the little lighter and often lay awake at night thinking about it.

"Was it wise to leave the mark this time?" she whispered, shuddering slightly. She had plenty of courage, but after all she was a woman, and a woman should not have too much nerve.

He laughed gently and threw an arm around her as he used his free hand to pull the false elevator door closed behind him. It was very dark in the big steel box when the light from the elevator was cut off by the closing of the door. Faintly they heard the elevator start into motion automatically upon the closing of that door.

Richard Wentworth continued his low laugh out of pure joy. A dead man behind him meant nothing. Nita was safe again, and he was in the middle of a great adventure. He was holding her now with both arms. Death had passed them by, and love had come. Those were the two great adventures for him, love and death.

"Dick!" she protested impishly. "Don't you think we could find a more appropriate place?"

"Right!" he returned, releasing her. "Let us first proceed to the further taking apart of Mortimer Mack."

CHAPTER 15
"RICHARD WENTWORTH IS
THE SPIDER!"

I N THE jet blackness of the steel box a slender beam of light shot out from a "fountain pen" flashlight which Wentworth had taken out of the fat, leather case which somewhat resembled a cigar case. It was one of several surprises which that case contained, surprises ingeniously constructed by the old professor. Perhaps no burglar ever had so compact a kit of tools, instruments which were constructed upon the smallest possible scale but with such ingenuity that they were of great power in the hands of so skillful a man as Wentworth.

Only a stab of light was necessary for Wentworth to find the bolt which held the door of the imitation safe. For the moment he had lost his sense of direction in the complete darkness. No man can kiss a lady in the dark and remain oriented. If he can, he doesn't know how to kiss.

Gently Wentworth pulled back the bolt and opened the door a very little. Light was burning in the study which appeared to be empty, but through the crack he could not see the entire room. He listened and, hearing nothing, took a chance by throwing the door wide and swiftly stepping into the room. The room was empty, but he glimpsed a flicker of green at the door. It might have been the flash of a woman's dress. It might have been Cora's emerald green dress, a bit of her clinging skirt as she stepped out of the room into the hall. If so, had she seen the opening of the steel door?

129

As Nita stepped out of the steel box, Wentworth closed its door and noted that it automatically locked itself. It could only be opened again, from the study, by means of the combination.

There might be other tricks to that dangerous study, but Wentworth believed that, for a few moments at least, they were safe. He took one of the books from a shelf and opened it with Nita beside him as though they were idly examining it.

"Now tell me," he said quickly in a low voice while he turned a page, "what became of Jerry Stone?"

She had, she told him, followed Jerry into the passage, but had not had to dissuade him from entering the study. He had hesitated at the door and then, plainly frightened, had bolted through the side entrance to the ballroom and on through that large room to the elevator, which he had entered. The car door had closed behind him before she could reach it.

She had then returned to the gambling salon and left it at once to enter the passage in her search for Wentworth, only to be captured at the study door by the unknown man who was now a dead passenger in an automatic elevator.

"Come on!" he exclaimed, closing the book when she had told him all she knew. "Let's hunt up Mortimer Mack and see what happens. He should be surprised to see us both alive and together."

But at the entrance to the gold-draped gambling salon it could be seen that something of a change had come over the room. Some of the guests had departed, leaving fewer at the table. And the table, itself, had changed. A smooth, white covering was upon it, and upon the covering, before the remaining guests, were a number of sets of dominos and jig-saw puzzles with which some of the guests were listlessly playing. The roulette table had been completely concealed, and the professional croupiers were no longer to be seen.

And the reason for this sudden change was in plain view. In the middle of the room, talking with Mortimer Mack, was Stanley Kirkpatrick, Commissioner of Police of New York City.

Probably Kirkpatrick would not be greatly incensed by a roulette table where there was no profit to the house, and where so much money was given to charity. But his official conscience had been eased by concealing from him the sight of so professional a table.

But why, Wentworth wondered, was the Commissioner of Police present? He was one of the most brilliant heads that the New York Police Department had ever had. He was one of the few high officials who was completely incorruptible and who lived up to his oath of office without thought of anything except his duty.

Richard Wentworth knew Commissioner Kirkpatrick well. He often dined with him and golfed with him and, frequently, fought with him over police work. And so highly did the Commissioner regard his friend, Wentworth, that upon one occasion he had paid him the dubious compliment of suspecting him of being the notorious "Spider."

Upon one occasion of this suspicion Kirkpatrick had very nearly caught his friend. By a remarkably clever deduction he had concluded that the mysterious killer must carry his tiny seal in his cigarette lighter. Immediately after a Spider killing he had forced his friend to hand over his lighter for examination, and it was only an adroit subterfuge on the part of Nita that hid Wentworth from exposure. Kirkpatrick, his suspicions put at rest, had apologized.

And now the Commissioner was actually present at the time and place of another Spider killing. If that killing were discovered, Kirkpatrick's suspicions would certainly be centered again upon Wentworth. The Commissioner was very astute and, in the line of duty, cared neither for friend nor foe. It might well be very awkward, even perilous for Wentworth.

BUT WENTWORTH advanced smilingly, with Nita upon his arm, to greet the Commissioner. Mortimer Mack turned as they came up, and Wentworth was certain that he started slightly upon seeing Nita.

Mortimer Mack, however, had full control of himself. He smiled at Wentworth and the girl and waved his hand to them.

"The Commissioner," said Mack lightly, "won't dance and doesn't care for the game of dominos."

"Dominos nothing!" retorted Kirkpatrick dryly. "You forgot to place some guests in the croupiers' chairs in the center of the table. I know a roulette table when I see one, even if it is camouflaged before I enter the room."

Nita, who knew the Commissioner almost as well as did Wentworth, placed a hand upon his shoulder. "Just one dance?" she suggested. "The orchestra is still playing in the other room and the floor is excellent."

"Sorry," returned Kirkpatrick, "but I'm here on serious business. Somebody sent me an anonymous message that the Spider would be here tonight and could be identified by the pistol which did one of the killings at Grogan's Restaurant yesterday. I didn't pay much attention to it until another message reached Headquarters anonymously that the politician, Buckley, had been killed here tonight. The two messages set me thinking and I thought I would look into the matter myself."

"I am sorry to disappoint you about Buckley," said Mack, smiling. "I believe that he left here about an hour ago."

"I telephoned his home ten minutes ago," returned the Commissioner, "and he had not yet reached it."

Mortimer Mack shrugged his shoulders and changed the subject. "As for the Spider," he said, looking straight at Wentworth, "I might be able to help you."

"What do you mean?" barked the Commissioner and his manner showed that he did not care a great deal for the little man who gave such elaborate entertainments. "Explain that remark, please."

"He means that I am the Spider."

To the astonishment of both Nita and Mortimer Mack the cool remark came from Richard Wentworth himself. He spoke indifferently, but with no show of facetiousness. Casually he took from his vest pocket the little lighter and leisurely lit a cigarette.

Stanley Kirkpatrick, unlike Mortimer Mack, showed no astonishment upon hearing Wentworth's startling remark. His face was expressionless, but his shrewd eyes gazed penetratingly at the man who toyed for a moment with his lighter before tucking it back into his vest pocket.

"I—I—" began Mortimer Mack and hesitated.

"Well, you what?" demanded the Commissioner. "I want to get to the bottom of this."

"I, too, received an anonymous message," continued Mack, regaining his fluency. "Somebody telephoned me that my guest, Mr. Richard Wentworth, was really the much-wanted Spider, the deadly killer of New York!"

THE COMMISSIONER frowned. "What evidence did he offer, Mr. Mack?" he snapped abruptly.

"He said that he had a witness to prove that Mr. Wentworth was in Grogan's Restaurant at the time of the double killing."

"In the meantime, before you put me under arrest, Mr. Commissioner," interrupted Wentworth smilingly as he began to fight back, "I would like to ask you if you came up here by means of the trick elevator which has so many strange secrets."

"Mr. Kirkpatrick entered this floor through the regular door which opens into the apartment house," volunteered Mack quickly.

"So?" from Wentworth. "Then Mr. Kirkpatrick will be interested in knowing that you have a very ingenious elevator which connects this floor with three more floors."

"Two!" shot back Mortimer Mack abruptly.

"Two!" Wentworth looked doubtful. "I thought I counted three other floors."

Wentworth's verbal attack was taking effect. Mortimer Mack was unable to conceal his uneasiness. He shifted a little from one foot to the other before speaking, and he shot a nervous glance at the Commissioner, who remained silent while his keen eyes saw much more of the hidden drama than would have been seen by the average man.

"This is ridiculous!" exclaimed Mack after a pause. "It has nothing to do with what brought the Commissioner here this evening."

"Suppose I explain the mechanism of the elevator to the Commissioner," suggested Wentworth, "and let him be the judge as to whether or not it is ridiculous."

"I should like to see this trick elevator," agreed Commissioner Kirkpatrick quickly. "Surely, Mr. Mack can have no objections."

There was a slight interruption. "Good night, Mr. Mack. I think I shall be going home." It was old David Bannister, the great publisher of newspapers, who had spoken. Not even Wentworth had heard him approach their little group in the center of the room. He seemed to shamble away again without waiting for any reply, but Wentworth noticed that he went toward the side entrance which opened into the passage that led to the study.

Mortimer Mack, a little hesitatingly, admitted that he had no objection to an inspection of his elevator. He suggested, however, that the Commissioner might like some refreshment before seeing it. Commissioner Kirkpatrick shook his head and, under Wentworth's guidance, moved toward the entrance hall where the red fires burned so dramatically. Behind them followed Nita with Mortimer Mack.

"Do me a favor?" asked Wentworth as they were crossing the room.

"What is it?" asked the Commissioner sharply, and Wentworth knew by his tone that he was again suspicious of him.

"If anything happens to me, take Nita safely home from here," said Wentworth in a voice so low that only the Commissioner could hear.

The Commissioner agreed readily enough to this request, and Wentworth knew that he could be depended upon. In the event of disaster to himself, Nita would be guarded by the most powerful man in New York City.

SEVERAL GUESTS were waiting for the elevator amid the twelve red fires. Commissioner Kirkpatrick stood in the middle of the room and regarded the hundreds of reflections, red fires and female forms, without showing any surprise or emotion. He turned directly toward the gilded woman and looked at her as he would have gazed at a statue. Strange female forms did not mean any more to him than they did to Richard Wentworth.

"Mr. Mack," he said dryly to the little man who was standing nervously beside him, "those women will die if they keep their pores covered with that stuff too long. Since there is no paid admission here, I won't interfere with you if you have 'em leave it off."

One of the waiting guests rapped on the door of the elevator. They were becoming very impatient and seemed to think that something had gone wrong with the car. They had never had to wait so long before.

Then the car arrived, and the door opened. Two ladies stepped in together. There were piercing screams and they staggered out again, clutching at each other for support. One of them slipped to the floor in a dead faint. A man peered into the elevator and drew back with a look of horror upon his face.

Commissioner Kirkpatrick strode forward and looked into the car. Upon its floor he saw a dead man. One eye had been shot out and on the cheek, beneath the ruined eye, was the vermilion outline of a tiny spider.

Commissioner Kirkpatrick held the elevator door open and barred the entrance with his arm. His face was cold and stern. A man, unnoticed before and evidently a plainclothesman, came quickly to his side.

"Case of homicide," rapped out the Commissioner. "Another 'Spider' killing. Telephone Headquarters and have the usual detail sent up." As the detective hurried away to obey the order, the Commissioner spoke again, still authoritatively. "Everybody will leave this room with the exception of Miss Van Sloan, Mr. Mack and Mr. Wentworth."

"By your special request," returned the Commissioner, "she is under my personal protection."

"Oh! Then you think that something has happened to me?"

Commissioner Kirkpatrick looked steadily into Wentworth's eyes before replying. "Mr. Richard Wentworth has too often been in the vicinity of the 'Spider' killing for it to be a mere coincidence," he said at last. "It will be necessary for you to be searched, and I intend to perform that act myself."

The guests and the female attendants had left the room as ordered, and the four of them were alone. Mortimer Mack fidgeted nervously, not knowing what to expect. Nita was tense but controlling herself. Wentworth, with a display of perfect indifference, took out his cigarette lighter and lit another cigarette. He held the little implement idly between his thumb and forefinger while he smiled at Mortimer Mack.

"I think that the Commissioner has found your elevator very interesting, Mr. Mack," he said quietly.

At sight of the cigarette lighter Nita had moved nearer to Wentworth, and he knew that she was maneuvering into a position where she could make some desperate attempt to relieve him of that incriminating article. Kirkpatrick, too, saw Nita's move and suspected her intention. A dead man in the elevator was forgotten for the moment by all save Mortimer Mack, who must have been sorely puzzled to know how the man's death had come about.

Commissioner Kirkpatrick held out his hand. "Let me have a look at that cigarette lighter, Wentworth," he said.

WENTWORTH SEEMED to be very much surprised at the request. But when the look of surprise died from his face, he demurred, while he continued to hold the lighter. Nita moved still nearer, and Kirkpatrick made his request for the lighter again, speaking more sharply.

Still Wentworth hesitated. He knew that the secret of the lighter was based upon a very delicate invention of the old professor, the dissipating of a fine film by contact with the air after the varnished junction had been broken. He continued to delay while he waited for something that nobody else had thought about.

138

Then the Commissioner of Police demanded and Wentworth could delay no longer.

"Nita?" asked Wentworth. "You want her?" his shoulders, indifferently, and with a trace of resignation upon his face, he handed over the lighter while Nita bit her lip and her heart beat fast.

There was some sorrow as well as sternness upon the Commissioner's face as he examined the junction which unscrewed to reveal the secret cavity. He had always liked Wentworth although he had suspected him upon several occasions. Into the palm of his hand he dropped the tiny seal from the cavity and seized it between thumb and forefinger, preparatory to making a print from it for examination.

It was then that the thing happened for which Wentworth had been waiting, the thing which the others had not expected. The elevator, with the front door open, began to descend. Under the influence of the master control, operated by an unseen hand, it began its descent in defiance of the ordinary control system.

Commissioner Kirkpatrick, preoccupied with the little seal, did not notice that the elevator had started until Wentworth unexpectedly brushed by him and stepped in. Then he saw that the car was in motion. Wentworth was fast disappearing.

The Spider was escaping! Desperately the Commissioner of Police reached for a gun in his pocket. But before he could draw it the elevator had vanished and Wentworth was gone with a dead man for his companion.

"How do you stop this thing?" demanded the Commissioner of Mortimer Mack, vainly trying to stop the car by pressing the button beside the open door.

"It—it must be out of order," lied the little man with every expression of truth upon his nervous face.

The Commissioner of Police had lost his composure for a few seconds. But he calmed himself very quickly and gently pressed the tiny seal upon the back of his own hand.

There, under his eyes a red print appeared…. But it was not the outline of a spider. He rubbed his eyes with his other hand and looked again. What he saw was a Line of four capital letters—NYPD. Old Professor Brownlee's delicate invention had worked.

"The initials of the New York Police Department," muttered the Commissioner to himself. "Well, I'll be damned!"

CHAPTER 16
THE SPIDER IN ACTION

RICHARD WENTWORTH, descending with a dead man for company, was at the mercy of the master control which guided the elevator. It was quite as he would wish. To be carried without effort into the unknown was adventure, and adventure was his life.

He closed the sliding door of the car so that the guests on the floors below might not glimpse what the car contained. From his pocket he drew the pistol which he had taken from the dead man and examined it. The magazine contained seven cartridges, and there was one in the barrel. He had eight shots with which to meet what might be ahead of him. They should be, he felt, sufficient.

Slowly the car passed the upper floor of Mortimer Mack's duplex apartment. Wentworth could faintly hear the buzz of voices from guests outside the elevator door. They did not interest him. He believed that he was going where guests were not admitted.

A smile suddenly crossed Wentworth's face as the car reached the next floor. It had suddenly occurred to him that never before had a murdered man been stolen from under the eyes of the Commissioner of Police of New York City. He did not doubt, however, that the city police would recover the body.

At that very moment, in all probability, patrol wagons and radio cars were beginning their rush toward the magnificent apartment building in which Mortimer Mack lived. In a very few minutes the huge building would be surrounded, and no corpse could be smuggled from it without detection.

As the car passed the lower floor of the duplex apartment and began its approach to the mysterious apartment below, Wentworth reached up and again unscrewed the little bulb which illuminated the interior. Once more he stood in darkness, while the elevator came to rest.

This time he did not wait but gently and quietly slid back the door, exposing a corridor which was in almost complete darkness. Only a little light came into it from an open door which was quite a distance from the elevator.

Acting upon the spur of the moment, as was so habitual with him, he pressed the starting button which would send the car

141

with its grim freight to the first floor above. Then he stepped out into the corridor and closed the door. Very faintly he could hear the elevator begin its ascent as the door closed. He smiled grimly as he visualized the consternation which would arise when some guest on the floor above discovered the dead man marked by the seal of the Spider.

He wondered, too, how long it would take the police to discover that the elevator had visited a floor still lower down.

In the distance, apparently from the lighted room with the open door, a telephone bell sounded. In the deep shadow of the hall Wentworth flattened himself against the wall, waiting to see if somebody would come to answer the telephone.

The bell stopped ringing,

Grogan screamed before the buckle cut into
his soft flesh: "She's at my restaurant, mister!"

and he knew that somebody in the room had lifted the receiver from the hook. Very quietly then, but quite quickly, he passed down the corridor until he stood close to the open door. Inside the room a man's deep voice was commenting angrily, viciously, over the telephone. And he recognized it as the voice of Dan Grogan.

Suddenly the man in the room crashed the receiver into its

cradle and rushed out into the corridor. He came so fast that there was no time for Wentworth to conceal himself. Then Dan Grogan, startled and scowling, came to a lurching halt as he looked into the muzzle of a pistol held by a man in evening clothes, a man who said nothing but seemed to smile very faintly as he indolently held the pistol.

"You're the guy that came down in the elevator once before," growled Grogan. "Whatcha doing here?"

Wentworth said nothing, but took a step forward. Grogan, growling, retreated nevertheless under the influence of the pistol, until he had returned to the room with the telephone. It was, Wentworth found, a bedroom, simply but well furnished.

"Get into bed," directed Wentworth abruptly, speaking for the first time.

"What?" gasped Grogan, amazed and indignant.

"You heard me."

Grogan sat on the edge of the bed. His eyes blazed with fury as he watched Wentworth feel behind him for the door, closing and locking it. The fury gave place to frantic fright as Wentworth raised the pistol and sent a bullet into the wall. The bullet passed so close to Grogan's ear that he threw himself to one side and lay gasping upon the bed. Outside of the apartment the report of the pistol must have sounded like the bang of a heavy door.

"I told you to get into bed," remarked Wentworth coldly.

Grogan scrambled to pull the counterpane up over him as fast as possible.

"Take your clothes off first."

This was almost too much. Dan Grogan's fat face looked out

from under the counterpane in wrathful bewilderment. But he scrambled out from under the counterpane and began to undress with desperate haste as Wentworth again raised the pistol. The manner of the man who confronted him was exceedingly unnerving. He acted as though he might shoot to kill without a second thought.

IN A few minutes Dan Grogan's big hulk exhibited its rolls of fat unadorned by any clothing. He pulled it hastily and clumsily under the counterpane in frightened silence. There was blasphemy in his mind, but he dared not speak.

Leisurely Wentworth, working with one hand and holding the pistol in the other, removed a picture from the wall and took off the wire by which it had hung. To Grogan's disgust and horror he jerked the counterpane from him and proceeded to bind his hands and feet to the four posts of the bed by means of the wire. Grogan protested, with the result that the wire was pulled tighter, cutting into the thick wrists and ankles.

Wentworth worked without speaking a word. His actions were so cold and deliberate that they were terrifying. Finally he stood at the foot of the bed, looking down at the gross body.

"Where is Molly Dennis?" he asked.

Grogan remained silent.

Wentworth stooped and withdrew the leather belt from Grogan's trousers where he had dropped them on the floor. With a mighty swing through the air he brought the buckle of the belt down in the very center of Grogan's fat stomach. The blow was severe, and the buckle cut through the skin, drawing blood.

Grogan groaned dismally and was quick to give an uptown address where he said that Molly was being held by some friends of his. He added that they were treating her very well.

Wentworth rested his hand upon the telephone. "I shall send a man to that address," he said in his cold, deliberate voice. "He will report back to me by telephone. If the girl is not there, I shall kill you. First I shall put a bullet through that fat stomach to give you a little pain…. After I lift this telephone you will die if you have not spoken the truth."

"Wait a minute'" Grogan half screamed under the influence of the threat which was made in such cold, slow words. "She isn't there, mister. I lied to you."

Wentworth, who knew that only brutality had any effect upon a man such as Grogan, swung the belt again. Once more the heavy buckle curved through the air and bit into the fat, heaving stomach, upturned upon the bed.

Dan Grogan writhed and groaned, but he was so utterly helpless that the fight was all gone from him. Wentworth had adopted this violent method of forcing the truth out of him for this very reason, knowing that it would be the quickest and surest way of doing it.

"Well, where is she?"

"She's where nobody can get her but me, mister. She's all right now, but they would croak her if anybody but me tried to get her." Grogan was speaking very earnestly and trying his best to make himself believed.

Wentworth's only answer was to swing the belt once more. The curving surface of the heaving stomach was becoming a

bloody mess, and Grogan's face was turning purple with suppressed resentment. He was afraid to express that resentment
in words, for fear of bringing down upon himself some even
more severe torture. The man, who stood above him, seemed
incapable of feeling any pity and appeared utterly fearless of
the consequences of anything which he might do. Murder was
in Grogan's heart, but he was physically incapable of the slightest retaliation.

Once more the threatening belt was raised, and this time
Grogan screamed before the buckle cut into his soft flesh.

"She's at my restaurant, mister!"

The words were forced out of him by fear and pain. He was
desperate and becoming very sorry for himself. Not remembering any of his own brutalities, he was considering only the
brutality which was being exercised upon him.

"I shall hold the telephone to your ear," said Wentworth.
"You will order her to be taken safely to my apartment within
one hour. I shall telephone my apartment at the end of an hour
and, if she is not there, I shall kill you."

GROGAN ONLY groaned in answer. The belt was raised
but did not descend as he commenced to speak.

"Let me up, mister, and I'll go with you and get her. There
isn't any other way. I can't telephone, because there isn't anybody
there to answer."

He seemed to be speaking the truth. Helpless and suffering
he had no courage left with which to lie, even if he possessed
the ability to lie successfully in the face of such a man as Wentworth.

The telephone bell began to ring. Without any hesitation Wentworth picked up the receiver from the little table beside the bed.

"Yeah?"

The one syllable was uttered in the deep, chesty voice of Dan Grogan. It was a beautiful imitation but, being only one syllable, was really quite easy. It was Mortimer Mack at the other end of the line, and Wentworth recognized the voice at once. Mack was speaking very fast and said that he had only a few seconds to talk. He said that the police might come down to the apartment at any moment.

"Yeah?" This time the one syllable was a deep, questioning growl, which carried with it suppressed hatred and surprise.

Swinging the belt idly with his free hand, Wentworth kept the telephone to his ear while he watched the cowed man upon the bed. Grogan, unable to move hand or foot, remained silent. There was nothing else for him to do unless he wanted to bring the belt buckle down upon himself again. He was quite convinced that the buckle might easily seek a more vulnerable part of him than his stomach. If it crashed into his face, something he had feared, there were his eyes to think about. Once he had gouged out a man's eye and had laughed, but his own eyes were quite another matter.

From upstairs Mortimer Mack continued to speak very rapidly, as if in fear of being interrupted at any moment.

"Richard Wentworth is here, the man who brought the girl to your restaurant," he said.

"Yeah!"

The single syllable, which Wentworth uttered at the mention of his own name, was a syllable of raging hatred.

"Get rid of Buckley through the other house," Mortimer Mack continued. "Then go back to the restaurant and get rid of the girl. She's too dangerous to hold any longer."

"Yeah! O.K.!"

This time Wentworth added two more syllables in the deep growl. He could imitate a voice so well that he might have said more, but he was taking no more chances than were necessary when so much was at stake. He thought that the conversation had ended, but there was something more, something so very important that it gave him new hope in connection with little Molly and her father who was in a death cell with the electric chair very close to him.

"And Grogan," Mortimer Mack's voice snapped, "don't forget that I have your confession for the Dennis killing. You will do as I say, or—"

Wentworth crashed the receiver down upon its cradle as a violent man might do if he were overcome with fury and could find no words with which to express himself.

"Where's Buckley?" snapped Wentworth, tossing the belt upon the floor and deliberately picking up Grogan's clothes and commencing a search of the pockets.

"Across the hall," returned Grogan in too much amazement to hesitate in his reply.

From one of Grogan's pockets Wentworth removed a small pistol, examined it briefly to see that it was in working order and dropped it into his tail pocket. There were no other weapons and he tossed the clothes upon the bed.

"Get up and get dressed," he ordered as he unfastened the wire which bound Grogan's hands. "We are going places."

DAN GROGAN was quick to unfasten the wire which bound his feet and to get into his clothes. He did not like to lie naked before a man who fired a pistol so carelessly, and who wielded a belt buckle with so little compunction. He felt that he would have at least a little more confidence in himself with his clothes on.

As a matter of fact Wentworth had denuded him of clothes for the very purpose of shaking his confidence and beating down his morale. A man, under our present day conventions, is weakened psychologically by being rendered naked.

Wentworth now had two pistols, one in his pocket and one in his hand. He toyed with the latter, watching Grogan hurrying to get dressed.

"Anybody else in this apartment?" asked Wentworth as Grogan finished dressing.

Grogan shook his head. "Not unless they came in after you did," he said.

Wentworth believed him. He was confident that the shot which he had fired so close to Grogan's ear would have brought somebody to the door of the room if there had been anyone else in the apartment.

He took up the telephone and dialed while Grogan was adjusting his collar and tie. In a few moments he was speaking in a way that made Grogan look over his shoulder in still more surprise. He was speaking Hindustani, which is not a language that is often heard in New York City, though there are, in the world, more people who understand it than there are people in the entire United States of America.

The conversation in Hindustani was brief. Wentworth turned to the man he had captured and who, because of the pistol in his hand, still remained a prisoner.

"How do we get out of here?" asked Wentworth.

"Well, there is the elevator," said Grogan. "You seem to know about that."

Wentworth informed his prisoner that the elevator was in the hands of the police of New York City and that they might use it to descend upon them at any moment.

"The cops!" exclaimed Grogan, startled again amid his state of amazement. "Say, who are you, mister?"

"You can call me Dick."

So much had happened that it seemed a long time since a flashy young man had told the proprietor of Grogan's Restaurant that he might call him Dick. Yet the actual elapse of time had been only a little more than twenty-four hours.

Grogan stared at Wentworth, and recognition slowly came into his eyes. At last he knew who this strange man was. Or did he know? He had heard that the strange man, called Dick, was really the fashionable Richard Wentworth, the man who had received so much attention in the newspapers for his adventurous expeditions in foreign countries and for startling detective work which he occasionally did with the police in New York City.

151

But Richard Wentworth had been to him only a name. Such a man never came into Grogan's Restaurant, and Grogan never visited drawing-rooms where such a man appeared.

"Dick!" Grogan exclaimed and then was silent, not knowing what to think or say.

"What other way is there of getting out of here?" asked Wentworth, tossing his pistol in the air and catching it with a deftness that was a threat to Grogan far more than any words.

Grogan said that there was the usual front door which opened into the apartment building. Wentworth replied that the police were in the building and that it would probably be impossible for them to escape in that way.

"Escape?" questioned Grogan. "You want to escape? Aren't you in with the police?"

Wentworth smiled and shook his head. "I'm only in with myself," he said. "Lead the way. Let's have a look at Buckley."

As he spoke there came, faintly through the window, the scream of a police siren. The great power and the cleverness of the New York Police Department was coming into play because of the astuteness of their remarkable head in paying a personal visit to the establishment of Mortimer Mack. With such a clever man in personal control of operations, there could not be long to wait before the members of the force would be overrunning every portion of the Mortimer Mack establishment, secret or otherwise.

"Hear the siren?" asked Wentworth as Grogan paused. "We've got to move fast."

"I don't understand it," complained Grogan, easing his shirt away from his wounded stomach.

"You don't need to understand anything," snapped Wentworth. "Do as you are told and lead the way to Buckley, or I'll begin shooting and work up from your feet till you are dead. Move!" DAN GROGAN moved. There was nothing else for him to do. With such a man as Wentworth, it meant abrupt death for him to refuse or rebel. Even the slightest argument was extremely dangerous.

Grogan unlocked the door and led the way across the hall into another bedroom. Wentworth followed him, pistol in hand and wary.

In the second bedroom the body of Buckley lay upon a bed where it had been roughly dumped. Instead of paying any attention to the corpse, Wentworth pulled open the drawer of a dresser. Inside, very neatly arranged, was a complete opium smoking outfit. He gave it but a glance and closed the drawer again.

"So Mortimer Mack uses this floor for allowing some of his favored guests to enjoy a little dope, eh?" he queried the sullen and badly puzzled Grogan.

Grogan only shrugged his shoulders in resignation. What did it all mean anyway? What did this man want, and what was he trying to do? He didn't know.

"Does he let them have the needle too?"

"Sometimes." Grogan admitted it sullenly. Wentworth turned to the dead man on the bed.

"You kill him?"

Grogan's face was a picture of the utmost rage. He could scarcely control himself. Probably he could not have done so if it had not been for the feeling of his shirt sticking to his stomach where the blood was congealing.

"Doesn't matter," continued Wentworth. "But he's dead—murdered. How are you going to get him out of here? The police will be here in a few minutes, you know."

Dan Grogan was so puzzled that he was bewildered. He simply did not know what to say or what course to pursue. He knew that his captor would torture him or kill him outright at the slightest provocation, and he certainly did not wish to give him any such excuse.

"What are you going to do with me, Mr.—Mr. Wentworth?" he asked at last.

"So you know me, eh?" The question was snapped. "It took a long time to get it through your thick head."

"Well, Mr. Wentworth, I can't understand it if you're not working with the police. What are you going to do with me if I do what you ask?"

"There isn't any question about you doing what I ask," retorted Wentworth. "How are you going to get this dead man out of here?"

"If the place is surrounded by police it can't be done, Mr. Wentworth," protested Grogan, beginning to raise his hands as an indication of utter helplessness on his part to do anything about it.

The rising hands stopped suddenly and fell as a bullet from Wentworth's pistol pierced the fat calf of Grogan's left leg. It was a pretty shot and well judged because of the slack of the trouser leg.

"All right!" groaned the big man in dismay as he leaned against the foot of the bed for support. "All right, Mr. Wentworth, I'll do it. Don't shoot again!"

"If you don't, I'll leave the two of you, dead together, for the police to find," retorted Wentworth, unconcernedly throwing the safety catch of the pistol off and on with his thumb.

Dan Grogan heaved his huge shoulders in utter resignation to what had befallen him. He knew very well that Wentworth was not bluffing and that he would do exactly as he said if his orders were not obeyed. He left the support of the bed, tested his wounded leg and limped slowly out of the room, followed by Wentworth.

"It's this way." Grogan said, turning away from the elevator and the front portion of the apartment.

SLOWLY, WENTWORTH followed his wounded prisoner down the corridor. The passage was long, and, counting his paces, he decided that it reached to the limits of the big apartment house.

At the end of the corridor Grogan turned into a room. Wentworth followed him and found the room to be fitted out as a small office such as a man might use for his own personal affairs. But a secret means of escape was recognized by Wentworth after a single glance around. Another high, steel safe stood against the far wall, which must, he judged, abut upon the next apartment building.

Wentworth remembered the similar safe at the top of the

elevator shaft and he remembered, too, the old iron box of a safe which sank through the floor of the back room in Grogan's Restaurant. Here was evidence of the same master mind controlling a gigantic plot throughout all its ramifications.

"Get busy!" directed Wentworth, indicating the door of the safe. "Open it up and let's get out of here. Commissioner Kirkpatrick's men may arrive at any moment."

"You'll have to carry the stiff down here," said Grogan, feeling his injured leg gingerly. "I can't carry anything with this leg."

"Open it up!" snapped Wentworth. "Of what good is a dead body?"

Helplessly Grogan began to obey. He fumbled at first with the dial of the safe, then began to turn it slowly and carefully. Suddenly his face went blank. A look of horror came into it.

"Geez!" he exclaimed. "I've forgot the first number!"

There was no doubt about him speaking the truth. The quick terror upon his face was convincing proof of it. That terror increased as he wondered if his enemy would believe that he was speaking truthfully.

"Try the first number that comes into your mind," ordered Wentworth quickly. "It may be the right one."

As Grogan hastened to obey a shout came from the corridor. Somebody, near the elevator at the other end of it, had called to somebody else. There was another shout in reply. The voices were authoritative and could mean but one thing... The police had arrived!

Under the cunning direction of Commissioner Stanley Kirkpatrick, they had already penetrated the secret of the automatic elevator. Had there been any doubt about it in Wentworth's mind, he needed but one glance at Grogan's trembling fingers to know that the shouts did not come from any of his friends.

Swiftly and silently Wentworth closed the door of the little office and turned the key in the lock. He watched Grogan nervously turning the dial of the safe and saw him fruitlessly pull upon the handle of the door when he had finished. The first number which he had chosen had been the wrong one. It might take a long time before the first number could be discovered by chance, and the situation was desperate for both of them.

In the extremity Wentworth directed Grogan to get away from the safe and to sit upon the floor with his back turned to him, warning him that he would plug him through the head if he moved before he was given permission to do so.

Before the safe, then, Wentworth seated himself. This was no old-fashioned iron box that could be opened easily, as had been the safe in Grogan's back room at the restaurant.

More voices were heard in the corridor and steps could be heard coming toward the little office.

"Give me one of the gats," suggested Grogan, "and we'll fight it out."

Wentworth did not reply. He knew that it was absurd to shoot it out, trapped in a room, with the whole New York police force. But aside from that, and infinitely more important, he had never killed a policeman and had no intention of doing so. Rather than that he would let them shoot him. But he was very busy. He had means other than pistols with which to fight.

THE SPIDER

FROM HIS pocket Wentworth took the fat, leather case and extracted from it a curious little ear piece which dangled from a thin, insulated cord. Attached to the cord were also a tiny battery and a very thin cuplike structure edged with rubber. He inserted the ear piece and pressed the thin cuplike structure against the surface of the safe door, where it clung by suction because of the rubber edging.

Quickly Wentworth began to turn the dial. He was using an ear-phone of the highest amplification which had ever been built to fit into so small a space. It was so delicate that he had once listened to a fly walking across a piece of tin foil. Now, as he turned the dial, he could listen to the inner mechanism with very little trouble.

Somebody in the corridor tried the office door and, finding it locked, rattled upon it. Grogan turned his head, against Wentworth's orders, and held out his hand pleadingly. He was begging for his pistol. Wentworth worked steadily at the dial. He already had the first number and believed that he could detect the other two more quickly than Grogan could be brought to the safe to work the combination by memory.

More voices, undoubtedly those of policemen, sounded outside the door, and someone lurched against the door with his shoulder. But the door held.

"Bring an ax!" one of the policemen shouted to another.

Wentworth worked on as calmly as if he had all the time in the world, but he worked swiftly nevertheless. He had the second number and was searching for the third and last one.

An ax crashed against the door of the office, and Grogan struggled to his feet, frantic with fear.

At last, as the ax crashed again, Wentworth found the last number. He pulled on the handle of the safe, and the huge door swung open.

Grogan, without any urging, passed into the safe while Wentworth removed his cunning listening apparatus and wiped the dial free of all finger prints.

Then it was that the deviltry, the mad spirit of audacity, came out in Richard Wentworth, the adventurer. He reached for the electric light switch and plunged the room into darkness. Twice he shouted for help in the soprano voice of a woman, then slipped into the safe and pulled the door closed, where it locked itself automatically....

The door of the safe had scarcely closed when the outer door fell inward under the impact of many sturdy shoulders, and half a dozen policemen rushed into the room, pistols raised, flashlights piercing the darkness. The electric light switch was found and the place was flooded with light.

But the room was empty. Neither the woman who had screamed nor anyone else was within.

One of the most baffling mysteries of police annals seemed to have occurred. Mystified detectives searched the room and examined the one window carefully.

Then Stanley Kirkpatrick, Commissioner of Police, stood in the doorway of the office. He was never far behind the firing line when he was on a case. Sometimes he was ahead of it. He stood expressionlessly in the doorway and listened to what his men had to say.

"Send for an expert to open that safe," he directed without any hesitation. "You will find the explanation there."

In the Commissioner of Police, Richard Wentworth had a difficult opponent to deceive or to defeat….

CHAPTER 17
THE DARK HOURS
BEFORE DAWN

WENTWORTH SHOVED the bulky Grogan ahead of him through the big steel box. At the rear of the false safe he found an opening concealed by heavy curtains. Through these they emerged into another room, which was apparently a part of an entirely different building.

Wentworth snapped on an electric light and looked at Grogan, who seemed to be completely subdued.

"Who owns this place?" he asked sharply. "Mortimer Mack."

"Hide-away?" Grogan nodded. "Uh-huh, and getaway."

"Grogan, you are becoming quite reasonable," said Wentworth with a smile. "I really should reward you. Would you like to bathe your leg in the bathroom? Remember, though, that my friend, Stanley Kirkpatrick won't take more than half an hour to get through that wall."

But Grogan, it proved, had no desire to stay longer than necessary in the vicinity. They left the apartment, which was quite empty, and took the elevator to the ground floor. It was a fairly large building, and the elevator man showed no surprise upon seeing them. Wentworth stood quite close to his companion, and Grogan felt no inclination to make a break or to offer any resistance. He was quite certain that so cool and desperate a man as Wentworth would not hesitate to shoot him down in an elevator, or anywhere else, if he felt the least desire to do so. Such was the result of Wentworth's harshness upon Grogan's brutal nature.

The doorman called a taxi, and Wentworth assisted Grogan, who was limping, to get in first. Only a few yards farther down the avenue a police emergency truck and several other police cars were drawn up near the entrance of the big apartment building which housed the establishment of Mortimer Mack. Several policemen and men who must be plainclothesmen were standing at the door of the building.

"What's going on in the next building?" Wentworth asked the taxi driver.

"Dunno, sir," the taxi man replied. "Looks like a police raid."

"Dear me!" exclaimed Wentworth as if dreadfully shocked. "Such a nice building for such a thing to happen in." He stood on the sidewalk for a moment, looking at the police activity, then called to Grogan in the taxi. "I say, Dan, shall we toddle over and see what the bally tamasha is about?"

Grogan's only answer was a grunt. He could not think of any appropriate reply.

"Ah, well, we'll read about it in the morning papers," said Wentworth regretfully. "Driver, take us to Grant's Tomb."

The driver had thought from the first that both his fares were a trifle drunk. He was sure of it upon being directed to take them to Grant's Tomb. Nobody went to that colossal monument, far up on Riverside Drive, during the small hours of the morning. Except in broad daylight, when a few sightseers stared at it, it was about the loneliest spot in New York City.

But his fares looked as if they had money, and the taxi driver stepped on the starting pedal as soon as Wentworth entered the cab.

It was quite a long drive to Grant's Tomb, and there was not much conversation in the taxi during the drive. Grogan had wanted to know why they were going to such a place and Wentworth had replied that it was an excellent place to commit a murder. He had also assured Grogan the murder could take place right there in the taxi at any moment if he attempted to offer the slightest resistance.

Grogan felt quite sure of it and began to suspect that his captor was insane. If he wasn't a crook and wasn't with the police, then what was he? There wasn't any other kind of a man within Grogan's scope of knowledge.

THE TAXI cut through Central Park at 86th Street and continued on, across the west side of Manhattan, to Riverside Drive where it turned north. It was that hour, between late night traffic and early morning traffic, when Riverside Drive had scarcely any traffic at all. Hardly a car passed them and, when they reached Grant's Tomb, there was not even a petting party parked within sight.

Below them the Hudson River lay almost shrouded in early morning mist and above them the sky was very dark without a star in sight…. As Wentworth had said, it was a very good place for a murder.

To Grogan's surprise Wentworth paid the taxi driver, and to his disgust he was ordered to get out of the cab. The taxi man shrugged his shoulders, took the money and drove away. It made no difference to him why his fares wished to visit Grant's Tomb at so unreasonable an hour. There were all kinds of people in New York.

Grogan, placing most of his weight on his good leg, sustained the pain in the other and glared at Wentworth who, with apparent absurdity, had nothing better to do than to take out his handkerchief and blow his nose.

The handkerchief, being quite large and white, could probably be seen at some distance. At any rate a car, parked at a nearby curve in the road, moved swiftly out swooped down upon them and purred to an abrupt stop before them.

It was Richard Wentworth's town car; and beside the chauffeur upon the front seat was Ram Singh, who stepped swiftly out and confronted his master.

"*Sahib?*" the boy questioned, asking for directions.

But Wentworth spoke first to his chauffeur. "Jackson," he said, "I'd drive the bus myself. You don't mind walking home?"

"Not at all, sir," returned the chauffeur, touching his cap before turning upon his heel and walking quickly away. He had never had a better master and was quite accustomed to his unusual and sometimes astonishing ways.

On the sidewalk in the darkness beside the towering monument the three men stood in silence while the chauffeur walked

163

away. Ram Singh did not know what was going to happen and did not care so long as he was with his beloved master. Neither did Grogan know, but he cared very much, not liking the look of things at all. Abruptly Wentworth spoke, but his words did not divulge his plans.

"Ram Singh, you have your knife?"

"Han, sahib!" ejaculated the Hindu in the affirmative, drawing a long blade from his sleeve.

"Think you could stick it in this bad wallah's stomach?" Wentworth asked with every appearance of being sincere.

"Han, sahib!" Ram Singh affirmed with considerable enthusiasm. "Him stick good!"

Grogan's eyes opened wide in horror. Never before had he been taken for a ride to face a Hindu with a long and ugly knife in the deep shadow cast by Grant's Tomb during the lonely hours of the morning.

"Take him up those stone steps and let him sit on a bench till I am ready for him," Wentworth directed. "Let him taste the tip of your knife if he is slow, and drive it into him up to the hilt if he disobeys you."

Grogan helplessly turned to do as Wentworth had indicated; and Ram Singh prodded him from behind with the knife, without waiting to see whether or not he was going to be slow. Grogan thought that the Hindu servant was quite as heartless as his cold-hearted master and he hobbled painfully up the steps, groaning and grunting.

Wentworth immediately entered his car, switched on the light in the tonneau and pulled down all the blinds. Quickly he undressed and dressed again in day clothes, which he took from a suit case on the back seat. In the suit case was also a shoulder holster which contained one of his most prized pistols, one with which he could spin a quarter dollar at twenty paces time after time. It seemed strange that there should also be a slender walking stick lying upon the back seat.

Having dumped his evening clothes into the suit case for Ram Singh to press and put in order, at some time when adventure was not so pressing, he extinguished the light, raised the blinds and stepped out of the car. He was far better equipped now for anything that might happen than he had been when he set out that evening, unarmed and in evening clothes, with Nita.

HE ASCENDED the stone steps buoyantly, swinging his light cane, until he reached the stone platform which surrounded the huge tomb. Dan Grogan, seated upon a stone bench with his injured leg stretched out before him, glared up at him while Ram Singh, knife in hand, stood a few paces to one side.... Ram Singh could throw his knife quite as well as he could thrust with it.

"Grogan," said Wentworth, "your game is up. You killed Mortimer Mack's partner; and I want the evidence that will take Molly's father out of the death cell."

Grogan remained silent, squirming uneasily upon the hard stone bench.

"I'll make you a sporting offer," continued Wentworth. "If you will sign a confession, I shall give you twenty-four hours to run from the police. That is my best offer, and you don't deserve it."

Grogan shook his head. "I didn't commit any murder," he said, "and, anyway, a confession secured under torture does not carry in court."

"I don't intend to torture you," Wentworth returned. "I intend—to kill you."

"Might as well die one way as another," replied Grogan. The pain in his leg was making him desperate and he was becoming resigned and obstinate.

Wentworth knew very well that a confession was no good if extracted by torture, and he was aware that Grogan could probably prove torture by means of his bullet-pierced leg and his lacerated stomach—if forced to do so to save his own life. As for killing him—Wentworth had never yet killed an unarmed foe.

But something had to be done with Grogan and Wentworth had planned that something when he had conversed over the telephone with Ram Singh and given that faithful servant the directions to meet him at Grant's Tomb.

There was just one door in the huge stone monument which towered so high into the sky, and Wentworth walked over to it now. The door was big and heavy and, of course, it was locked and would remain locked until the caretaker came none too early in the morning.

It was not, however, a very difficult lock, and Wentworth succeeded in opening the door with one of those keys with which he was so adept.

"Bring him over," he called to Ram Singh.

Ram Singh prodded the bulky Grogan into motion and brought him to where Wentworth stood. Together they shoved the reluctant and almost stupefied man into utter blackness of the great tomb. Then the door was closed and locked again. For several hours at least, Dan Grogan would be utterly helpless and quite harmless to all the world.

He could not possibly get out and his loudest shouting would not be heard by anybody until the door was opened in the morning. True he was wounded and he would suffer. But his suffering was nothing in comparison to the suffering he had caused many people both physically and mentally.

RICHARD WENTWORTH'S objective now became Grogan's Restaurant. The master of that dingy establishment would not, of course, be present to receive him. There would, however, probably be others there and, in any case, the problem before him was far from an easy one.

Seated beside his master on the front seat, while Wentworth drove the car, Ram Singh felt his long knife where it fitted snugly into the sheath which was sewn inside his sleeve. He had not been able to use it, except just a bit of the point where Grogan was accustomed to sitting down. But the night was not over, and there was much hope in his breast for better things to come.

Ram Singh was not overly blood-thirsty, but he believed that real men belonged to the warrior cast; and, although he could cry over an injured kitten, he liked to kill—in a good cause. And was not Wentworth *sahib's* cause always a good cause?

They swept southward on Riverside Drive at a high speed. There was practically no traffic to delay them and it was at that time in the morning when the traffic lights were not in operation. Passing Riverside Mansions, one of the largest apartment buildings on the drive, Wentworth looked up at the high tower where Nita had her little apartment and noted that her windows were dark.

Half a dozen blocks farther on he saw a car approaching at a rate of speed almost as high as his own. The approaching car was escorted by two motorcycle policemen. Then Wentworth knew that the car belonged to the Commissioner of Police and that he was bringing Nita home in safety as he had promised. He wondered if Nita would recognize his car as they passed— glimpse Ram Singh or read the number plate.

And Nita did just that. Leaning idly back beside the Commissioner she saw the approaching limousine and just as the two cars were passing, her eye caught sight of Ram Singh's dark face and straight figure. She could not help giving a little start and leaning toward the window to look out. Although she leaned back again very quickly, her action had not been unnoticed by the alert Commissioner.

Commissioner Kirkpatrick, whose mind was as sharp as a knife edge, jerked his head around and looked back through the rear window. In another moment he had the speaking tube in his mouth and their car began to slow its furious speed to an abrupt stop. The motorcycle officers, not expecting the sudden stop, shot a long way ahead, but turned and came roaring back to find out what was the matter.

"Catch that car and bring it back to me," directed the Commissioner, pointing.

With a mighty roar from their exhausts the two motorcycle officers swooped away upon their mission.

Nita bit her lip. "Why do you want that car!" she asked, though she knew the answer.

"My dear," replied the Commissioner, "there is only one car in New York City that would make you bend forward tonight the way you did. That is Dick Wentworth's car."

THERE WAS some silence while they waited for the motorcycle men to return with the car after which they had been sent.

"Surely you don't think that Dick is guilty of anything," Nita said at last.

"I have known Dick since he was a boy," the Commissioner answered, "and I know how deucedly clever he is. Only such a man could play the Spider and elude me for so long."

"Of course you know that the Spider never hurt any man who was fit to live," she retorted. "Don't you think that Mortimer Mack is the guilty man, and that Dick is only a very reckless bystander?"

Commissioner Kirkpatrick agreed that there was a lot surrounding Mortimer Mack to make him suspicious, but he insisted that there was no proof of guilt. All the trick entrances and exits through walls and unsuspected lower apartment had been explained by Mortimer Mack as devices by which he conducted illusional effects for the entertainment of his guests. Artists and troops of entertainers were thus brought in surprisingly and made to vanish miraculously. As for the two murdered men, Mortimer Mack had simply shrugged his shoulders and claimed that the thing was as much a mystery to him as to anybody else. He even hoped that the Commissioner would solve the mystery and punish the guilty parties....

And in the meantime Wentworth had been quite as quick-witted as the Commissioner of Police. Looking back in his rear view mirror, he had seen the Commissioner's car stop and he had seen and heard the motorcycles as they began their frantic rush after him.

But the speed at which the two cars had been traveling in opposite directions gave him a big start. He guessed exactly what had happened and turned sharply eastward on a side street. His car, under the drive of its powerful engine, leaped forward in the middle of blocks and slowed just enough to make turns at corners as he zigzagged over to Broadway and ran south on that great thoroughfare.

For a few blocks he continued to look back, and, seeing no motorcycles behind him, turned west again to Riverside Drive and retraced his course on that drive at a furious rate until he slowed and stopped immediately behind the Commissioner's car.

"Want to see me?" he asked, getting out and coming to the window of the Commissioner's car.

"If I did, I have changed my mind," said the Commissioner, believing that Wentworth would never have come back if he had had any evidence of guilt upon him. He smiled. "Don't you see I am taking a lady home? Get out of here and leave us alone."

Wentworth grinned at Nita and lit a cigarette from the Commissioner's automatic lighter just inside the window. "Any spiders on this lighter of yours, Commissioner?" he asked.

"Get out!" roared Kirkpatrick with a broad smile. "I'll put you at the head of my detectives if you will join the force."

"Not enough excitement in it," drawled Wentworth. "By the way, shall I find your motorcycle escort and send them back to you?"

"Go to the devil!" the Commissioner exclaimed, laughing and signaling to his driver to move on without waiting for the escort. To Nita, who had been highly amused, he added as their car moved off: "You can't help liking that fellow—even if he does sometimes make a monkey of you!"

CHAPTER 18
GOING DOWN!

THE SIDE street, upon which was located Grogan's Restaurant, seemed quite deserted when Wentworth and Ram Singh entered it after leaving their car just around the corner. There was no traffic upon the road and not a pedestrian was to be seen. The blinds of the restaurant were closely drawn and there was no light visible from door or windows.

Only a mangy white cat greeted them as they approached the door. And the animal ran ahead of them and stood expectantly at the door for it to be opened.

"Seems as if somebody was inside, or the cat wouldn't do that," commented Wentworth.

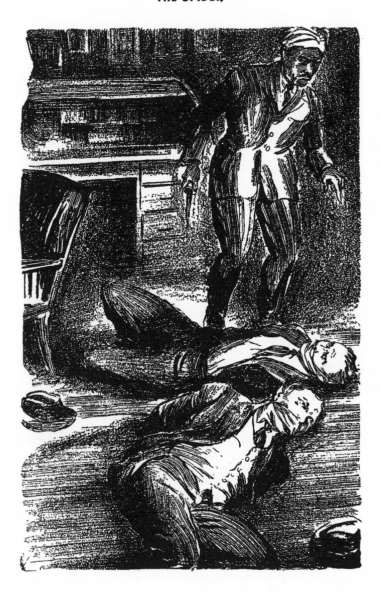

Quickly Wentworth stepped upon the safe, gun in

hand, as it disappeared through the floor.

He tried the door and found that it opened. The cat, tail up, marched in ahead of them.

The dingy restaurant seemed more sordid than when he had visited it before. A man and a woman, both drunk, were trying to improve their condition with ham and eggs, and it did not seem as if the ham and eggs would have much chance against the alcohol. Distinct snoring issued from one of the curtained booths; and from the other could be heard some very drunken and profane conversation. Lastly, the door of Grogan's back office was ajar, and from it masculine voices were audible.

A sleepy waiter came forward to take Wentworth's order. He was the same man who had served Wentworth before. But he showed no sign of recognition. Indeed it would have taken a very discerning person to have identified the present customer with the man who had the flatly plastered hair on the former occasion.

"Ham and eggs," said Wentworth. "And a saucer of milk for the cat."

The order of milk for the cat brought a titter from the drunken woman, with the result that she got a punch on the jaw from her escort. In return she threw the sugar bowl at the man and screamed at him in the filthiest kind of language.

However the sugar bowl missed its mark and her screaming soon exhausted her so that she quieted down. Nobody paid any attention to the episode except the waiter who picked up the sugar bowl, scooped up the lumps of sugar from the floor and put them back in the bowl. This was Grogan's Restaurant.

Of course Wentworth had no expectation of finding little

Molly Dennis in the visible portion of the restaurant. But he did expect to find her in some part of it which was not open to public observation, probably underneath the back office where the iron safe sank from view on its descending platform. How he would reach that place he did not yet know. It might be by force, and it might be by craft.

The waiter brought the ham and eggs for Wentworth and a bowl of bean soup for Ram Singh, who seldom ate meat and never any ham. The cat, too, was given its saucer of milk and proceeded to lap it up greedily.

Indeed the cat finished his milk very quickly and stalked over to the drunken woman to beg for more food. The woman bent down to pet the cat and fell out of her chair, with the result that the cat fled through the partly open door into the back office.

Instantly Wentworth seized the opportunity which was offered him. He rose and followed the cat. Shoving the door farther open, he entered the back office just a bit unsteadily. Two men were seated by Grogan's desk and a third man lay bound and gagged upon the floor. The third man, in a rumpled dinner coat, was Jerry Stone!

WENTWORTH FROWNED uncertainly. "You got my cat?" he asked, rocking a little as he stood by the door.

"Cat?" questioned one of the men in astonishment "Who the hell told you to come in here?"

The white cat had walked over to the bound man and was gingerly sniffing at him. Anything strange interests a cat, and bound men upon the floor are not usual.

"There's my cat!" exclaimed Wentworth, making a quick dive toward the animal.

But the cat was alarmed by his quick move and ran behind the desk, followed by Wentworth. Now a man who chases a cat at four o'clock in the morning in a restaurant should not be very dangerous. One of the men laughed and the other told him to take his damned cat and get the hell out. Then they both realized that this stranger had seen the bound man upon the floor. One of them went to the door and closed it.

"Who are you?" this man asked.

"Name is Dick," Wentworth replied and, as he spoke, a pistol seemed to appear magically in his hand.

The other man sprang to his feet and joined his comrade by the door, where they both remained motionless while the muzzle of the little weapon circled and darted like the head of a snake between the two of them.

"Now listen, you two," said Wentworth and there was no sign of unsteadiness as he faced them from behind the desk. "Grogan is pinched and Mortimer Mack sent me here to take a look at what you are doing."

"Grogan pinched!" exclaimed one of the other men in dismay, while the other was too astounded to speak.

"You leave the door open," continued Wentworth, "and let a crazy man chase a cat in here. You let him see Jerry Stone where you have him tied up on the floor, and then you let him get the drop on you as if you were a couple of boys!"

With supreme audacity Wentworth put away his pistol, lit

a cigarette and sat upon the desk, swinging his legs as if he had not a care in the world.

It was then that the telephone sounded upon the desk. Wentworth picked up the receiver without any hesitation and quiet as if it were his own office.

"Yeah?" he questioned in the deep voice that he had used before when impersonating Grogan.

And once more it was Mortimer Mack's voice that came to him from the other end of the wire. Mack was very pleased to hear Grogan's voice and to know that he had gotten safely away from the police raid. He wanted to know if everything was all right at the restaurant.

Wentworth answered with the single syllable of affirmation and added an O.K. in the same voice. His easy manner of perfect assurance was impressing the two men who were watching him closely.

Mortimer Mack said that they were going to get rid of the Commissioner of Police on the following evening and that after that everything would be smooth sailing again, as the next Commissioner would be a man that the politicians could handle. He, Grogan, was to hold himself in readiness to be on hand for the ending of Commissioner Kirkpatrick.

"Yeah? Where?" asked Wentworth.

"At David Bannister's home," answered Mack.

"O.K.!" was Wentworth's answer, and the conversation ended.

The cat had again gone back to Jerry Stone for another gentle sniffing; and the two men stared in silence at the man who still sat carelessly upon the desk.

177

"Now, you mugs," Wentworth said at last. "That was Mortimer Mack talking to me. He wants me to bring Jerry Stone and the girl, Molly, up to his place. Get the girl ready, and I'll look after Stone."

Wentworth slipped from the desk and knelt beside Jerry Stone, deliberately commencing to untie the bindings.

"Wait a minute!"

From the floor Wentworth turned and looked up into the muzzle of a gun which one of the men held. The other was at the telephone.

"I'll just confirm what you say by phoning Mack, myself," said the one at the telephone, while he dialed.

OUTSIDE IN the restaurant Ram Singh had eaten his bean soup. He had been very busy with it when his master had left the table in search of the cat. It was quite all right with him if his master wished to chase cats. But when the door of the back room had been closed and neither his master nor the cat came out again, Ram Singh decided that he had better go and assist in the cat hunt.

Consequently the man who threatened Wentworth with the pistol was very much astonished when Wentworth knocked the weapon out of his hand with an adroit blow, while Ram Singh placed the point of his knife against the back of the man who held the telephone.

After that it was a very simple matter and a very quiet one. The people in the restaurant would have heard nothing even if they had been sober.

In a very few minutes Jerry Stone was unbound and free,

while the two men were bound and gagged and stretched out in his place upon the floor. When Wentworth and Ram Singh worked together, things were done with very great efficiency.

Jerry Stone, it seemed, had been sent down to the restaurant upon some plausible errand only to be seized and bound because they had found out that it had been he who had notified the police of Buckley's murder.

"But why did you notify the police?" asked Wentworth.

"I thought that, if the police discovered the murder, I could threaten to give evidence that Grogan did the shooting unless Mr. Mack in some way got Molly's father out of jail," young Stone answered. "You see, Mr. Wentworth, all the time I have been letting them use me so that I could get something on them."

As Jerry Stone finished speaking there was a slight creaking sound. And in another moment the cause of that sound became apparent.... The old iron safe was slowly sinking through the floor!

"What is down there?" asked Wentworth quickly.

Jerry Stone shook his head. "I don't know for certain," he said, "but I think that's where Molly is."

Quickly Wentworth stepped to the top of the safe and squatted upon it—gun in hand—as it *disappeared through the floor!*

CHAPTER 19
THROUGH THE FLAMES

I T WAS a novel situation, even for Richard Wentworth, to be seated upon an old iron safe which slowly descended through the floor of the back office of so disreputable a restaurant. It might seem to be a reckless act. But it was probably the last thing which his enemies would expect him to do, and it was by doing the unexpected thing that he often won success. Nevertheless he knew that danger might be met in the unknown, and his senses were keenly alert as the safe descended into almost complete darkness.

Some light came through the aperture in the floor above as the safe came to rest and the mechanism ceased its vibration. But there was not enough for him to see what the place contained nor the walls which surrounded it. He saw the face of Ram Singh peering down from above and knew that his retreat was well guarded.

With Grogan safely locked up in Grant's Tomb, he felt confident that Ram Singh could hold the room above against any attack, at least until he had time to climb back through the hole and join him.

But what of the place he was in? In order to remove himself from the faint light which descended from the hole above, he slipped quickly off the safe and crouched, motionless, in the dark a little to one side. He found himself standing upon what seemed to be a cement floor covered with straw.

Gradually, as eyes became more accustomed to the darkness,

he was able to distinguish vague outlines of boxes. In addition, he discovered a faint line of light close to the floor. That line evidently came from beneath a door which must open into a room below the kitchen.

For some few minutes Wentworth remained perfectly motionless while he bent every effort to listen. Several times he thought that he could distinguish breathing near him and once more the straw rustled. Of course the rustling of the straw might have been caused by a rat. But, unless the rat had asthma, he did not believe that he could hear its breathing. Again he heard what seemed to be a faint indrawn breath and again the straw rustled slightly. He was confident that someone was in that dark room, not more than a few feet away.

Very quietly he drew a flashlight from his pocket, but delayed using it until he had learned a little more by means of his ears. In his other hand he held his pistol, ready for use if the flashlight revealed any immediate threat.

Above him the drunken woman was trying to sing a sentimental song and a chair scraped on the restaurant floor.

Suddenly the voices of the two men became audible. They were arguing excitedly, on the other side of the door below which the line of light appeared.

"You shouldn't of lowered the safe," one of them argued. "You can't open it, and you'll get bloody hell."

"Maybe I can work the combination," the other returned excitedly. "I've got to get a sniff of the stuff, or I'll go nuts!"

The other man swore, said he would have nothing to do with

it and that he was going back to the kitchen. "Grogan will be back any minute, and I know what's good for me," he added.

The brief dialogue told the entire story of why the iron safe had been lowered to the dark room below. A wretched drug addict, dying for a pinch of heroin, had lowered the safe in the slight hope that he could work the combination and obtain some of the drug to relieve his nerves.

Very soon the door would probably be opened and the presence of an intruder would be discovered. Of course a drug addict is not a very formidable antagonist except that he may be exceedingly rash and will kill, if he has the chance, without any hesitation. He is, however, at a great disadvantage when matched against a real fighter with steady nerves. Wentworth was quite confident that he could handle such a man, either by wit or by force. But he did not want to meet him before he knew who it was that was breathing so close to him.

It was then that the accident happened which might easily have ended so disastrously. Without any warning his flashlight was knocked from his hand. He was robbed of the one means which would show him instantly who and what was near him.

Instantly he raised his pistol to strike, not caring to fire at an unseen person. And with his free hand, the hand which had held the flashlight, he reached swiftly forward to seize what might be before him, so that he could strike accurately in the dark.

HIS REACHING hand grasped rough cloth beneath which was a shoulder. The raised pistol commenced to descend upon the place where the head should be.

Then it stopped! Never before had his wit acted more quickly to save him from making a mistake. The shoulder was so small that it could only be that of a boy—or a girl!

But if Wentworth stopped his attack, his antagonist did not. Small hands beat upon him, striking his head and chest wildly. Hard little boots began kicking and found his shins as often as they missed. He could not bring himself to beat into uncon-sciousness so small an antagonist and he could not run away. The only remaining course was to come to closer quarters. He dropped his pistol into his side pocket and seized the boy or girl in his arms.

It was a girl. He discovered that just as soon as he lifted her from the floor. And he discovered more. The coarse coat and ragged trousers confirmed what he had suspected. In the dark he was holding little Molly Dennis, still dressed in the street urchin's clothes which she had worn when he had taken her back to Grogan's Restaurant. "Molly!" he whispered. "Be still! This is your old pal, Dick Wentworth."

But she was too frightened and excited to hear him, or at least to understand. She fought on, trying to slap and scratch.

And then there was light. The door into the next room was open, and a man was standing in the doorway with an oil lamp in his hand.

Wentworth, struggling to hold Molly so that she could not scratch him and at the same time so as not to hurt her, caught a second glimpse of the man with the oil lamp. In the man's other hand was a pistol, one of those ugly little things which are so short that they can be concealed in the palm of the hand and which are made for cowardly killings at very short range.

There was nothing for Wentworth to do except to drop Molly. In the first place he had to get her out of harm's way as much as possible, in case the man opened fire. In the second place he had to let go of her in order to get at his own pistol.

It was just as he dropped her that she recognized him and, instead of getting away from him, she came close to him. Her face was even dirtier than when Ram Singh had so cleverly made it up, and it was both saucy and bewildered as she looked up at him.

"Oh!" she exclaimed. "I didn't know it was you." She began to smile whimsically and looked at the man with the lamp and the pistol as if he did not matter at all. "Now everything will be all right," she said softly.

But Wentworth shoved her away from him with one hand, hoping that her optimistic belief was well founded. The man was trembling so that both the gun and the lamp were shaking. He was desperately in need of his drug, and his nerves were shot to pieces. His twitching finger might discharge the weapon accidentally at any moment, or he might take it into his head to shoot out of pure viciousness.

"Whatcha doing here?" the man demanded, keeping his pistol pointed at Wentworth.

"Came down here to get some snow," replied Wentworth quickly. "Grogan's away and I know how to open the safe."

The man looked eager, but hesitated while Wentworth considered the advisability of attempting a quick draw. If his pistol had been in its holster, he could have drawn and fired with confidence. But he had dropped it in his side pocket, and it is almost impossible for a man to pick a pistol out of his side pocket quickly enough, when his opponent has him covered.

Even so, Wentworth might have attempted it, if it had not been for Molly. If anything happened to him, it was almost certain that she would meet with disaster. Certainly her father would give his life for a crime which had been committed by another man.

"Go ahead!" ordered the man after a pause. "Open the safe if you can do it."

"Hold the lamp by the dial," replied Wentworth, knowing quite well that he could disarm the drug addict with ease if he could get close enough to him.

But although the man was now a pitiful addict, he was, or had been, one of the underworld killers and he knew his trade. He shook his head and said that there was enough light from where he stood.

Wentworth approached the safe and began to twist the dial of the combination. He knew that Ram Singh was watching from above but, unfortunately, the addict continued to stand in the doorway, from which position he could not be seen through the hole in the floor above. Wentworth could have called his servant, who would unhesitatingly have dropped through the hole to come to his assistance, but would certainly have received the first bullet from the man's pistol. Although Wentworth could then have fired the next shot and ended the matter, he would not sacrifice his servant to save himself.

There was one more probability which had to be taken into consideration by Wentworth while he slowly turned the dial. It was probable, almost certain he believed, that the man would shoot him down as soon as he opened the door of the safe. Everything being considered, it was necessary that this man should be disarmed or killed at once. And Wentworth had to do it himself.

HE CONSIDERED the matter and came to a decision during the last few seconds that he was twirling the dial. He was working with his right hand but, as a pistol shot, he was ambidextrous and, if anything, shot a little better with his left hand than with his right.

Slowly his left hand, the unsuspicious hand, crept into his side pocket and gripped the pistol. Then suddenly he seemed to rise in the air as he sprang away from the safe.

Crack! The little pistol of the drug addict barked. There was a roar in reply, as Wentworth fired while at the very height of his bound into the air. The other man's bullet missed by an inch or so, but the heavy shot from Wentworth's gun struck the addict in the shoulder. The wounded man lurched backward through the open door, as the lamp he had held dropped with a crash upon the floor....

Such was the cause of the great fire at Grogan's Restaurant—the fire which wiped out every vestige of the evil place and left the firemen playing their hose upon a mass of glowing embers. The oil lamp broke, and the oil, igniting, ran into a heap of straw at the base of a pile of wooden boxes which had once contained dope of various kinds. The room, once so dark, was ablaze in a very few seconds, and there was nothing available which could possibly extinguish the flames.

Wentworth realized the danger immediately and leaped for Molly. Behind his back he heard the slamming and locking of the door which opened into the next room, the only exit except the square hole in the floor above. And, as he picked her up, slight and fragile, he heard something still more ominous. He heard the grating of the mechanism which lifted the heavy safe. From the next room the drug addict had started the machinery which would lift the iron safe and block the hole above!

As quickly as possible he carried the girl to the rising safe and reached it just in time. He lifted her up and placed her on top of the safe when there was just sufficient room to do so without having her crushed as the heavy iron box entered the square hole.

"Ram Singh!" he called through the last few inches of space. Defend her with your life and take her to Van Sloan *missie sahib!*"

As the safe slid into the aperture, very faintly but very earnestly the reply came to him: *"Han sahib!"*

While the heat of the flames beat upon his face, he knew that the Hindu would carry out that last order of his at the risk of his life, if a long knife and muscles of steel could accomplish the task.

But was it his last order? Wentworth was almost surrounded with leaping flames, and the only two exits were barred. The heat was almost unbearable and becoming greater. In that inferno life could only continue for a very few minutes longer.

187

The door into the next room was on fire, but it could not possibly burn down in time to save his life.

He seemed to be hopelessly trapped and, in the center of the room where he was farthest from the flames, he quietly laughed to himself. So this was the end. The next adventure would be death, the greatest adventure of all!

THAT LITTLE laugh seemed to do Wentworth good. He came very abruptly into action again. He would be damned if he would be beaten. There was just one chance. He lifted his pistol again. There were seven cartridges left in the magazine and one in the barrel. From the center of the room he fired eight shots into the lock of the door, placing them all within the diameter of a fist. Then, with a great spring, he threw himself, right shoulder first, into the door.

The door gave way and fell into the next room with Wentworth on top of it, his hair singed and his clothes smoking. Bruised but vigorous, he picked himself up, climbed a rickety, narrow stairs and found himself in the kitchen. Here there was as yet no fire, but the room was filled with smoke and, in front, the restaurant was a mass of flames.

The back window of the kitchen was open and belching smoke into a small fenced yard. With the smoke Wentworth climbed through the window and dropped to the ground outside. It was a matter of only a few minutes for him to scramble over the fence and race along a lane to the street.

He reached his car just as Ram Singh was lifting Molly into the tonneau, having refused to put her down for one instant from the moment that he had snatched her from the top of the rising safe while the fire was eating through the floor upon which he stood.

But he dropped her abruptly upon the floor of the car as his master touched him on the shoulder.

"Khudda bara hai!" exclaimed Ram Singh emotionally, while tears of joy streamed down his face.

"Yes, God is great," agreed Wentworth, smiling while he slipped unconcernedly into the driver's seat. "But He favors those who help themselves."

CHAPTER 20
MURDER MASQUERADE

I T WAS the following evening, just as dusk was falling, that Richard Wentworth sat with Nita Van Sloan on the window seat of Nita's tower apartment in Riverside Mansions. Apollo, the Great Dane, sat upon the floor with his massive head upon the seat between them. The dog did not know which of them to favor, so he placed his head midway between them and looked up, first at one and then the other.

They had not spoken for some little time, so much in sympathy, or in love if you like it better, were they. Below them the mighty Hudson flowed outward to the sea and upon its far shore, lines of twinkling electric lights were beginning to gleam along the crest of the majestic Palisades. Such moments of silence with Nita and the dog, high up above the mighty scene, were almost as precious to Wentworth as were his moments of strife and adventure. His nature swung to the two extremes, permitting each to be attained the more intensely.

At last he broke the silence. "Nita," he said, "I think you had better not come with me tonight. It may be more dangerous than we think."

She made a little face at him and shook her head obstinately. "We can't be married because you are too wild, old boy," she retorted. "Therefore I am going to do a little bossing without the ceremonial authority. Tonight I'm going with you and that's that!"

"Well," he returned, "I have made all arrangements for it if you insist, but you don't know what you are letting yourself in for. You are going to have the surprise of your life."

And so it was that they took the long elevator ride down to the ground floor of Riverside Mansions and found Wentworth's motor car waiting for them at the door, with Ram Singh seated beside the chauffeur in front. Without any direction from Wentworth the car moved off as soon as they had entered and turned south, running to 59th Street and stopping, still without any directions to the chauffeur, at one of the southern entrances to Central Park.

Wentworth glanced at his watch, turned on the light in the tonneau and pulled down all the blinds. He lifted a small suit case from the floor and handed it to Nita.

"Here is your costume," he said. "Put it on while I drive once around the park."

The chauffeur stepped out of the car and lit a cigarette while he leaned against the wall of the park near the entrance. Wentworth took his place at the wheel and drove into the park. Ram Singh sat up very straight beside his master and said nothing, knowing that everything was planned for the evening, up to a certain point. Beyond that point no one could tell what might happen. In the meantime, there was nothing to discuss.

In the tonneau of the car Nita opened the suit case and found one of the cheapest and most vulgar evening dresses she had ever seen. At no time had she ever worn such a thing. She was beginning to understand what Wentworth had meant when he said she was going to have the surprise of her life. Shielded from view by the drawn blinds, however, she undressed to her very dainty undies and dressed again in the very flashy concoction which she took out of the suit case and was amused because it fitted her so well. Wentworth had an amazingly accurate eye for the female form.

The car circled the park at a high rate of speed and returned to the same southern entrance. Wentworth descended from the driver's seat and the chauffeur tossed his cigarette away, left the wall and resumed his seat. Ram Singh also left the front seat and, together with Wentworth, entered the tonneau. All this was done without a word of direction, so carefully was everything planned. Again the car moved off, under the guidance of the chauffeur, to circle the park once more.

In the tonneau, still shielded from view by the drawn blinds, Ram Singh opened his little make-up box.

Nita, puzzled, surprised and amused, submitted her face to the work of Ram Singh's nimble fingers. Rapidly her features changed and her face became flamboyant, painted beyond the limits of woman's oldest profession. It was quite unlikely that even Wentworth would have recognized her if he had passed her on the street.

"I'm sorry, my dear," said Wentworth, "but Ram Singh has to make you the exact opposite of yourself in order to give you a perfectly safe disguise."

She looked at herself in the little mirror, which Ram Singh reluctantly held up, and gasped.

"And what about you?" she asked. "What kind of a terrible character are you going to be?"

For answer Ram Singh commenced his work upon Wentworth. But it proved a comparatively simple transformation, and occupied much less time than had Nita's make-up. The skin was lightened so that he became pallid and had the appearance of being rather undernourished. What appeared to be a grease smudge was run from ear to chin in such a subtle way that he appeared to be partly comical and partly pathetic.

To complete his disguise Ram Singh handed Wentworth a long linen coat. It was very dirty and had once been yellow. It buttoned tightly around his throat, completely covering his dinner coat, and reached almost to his feet. A cap, slightly too large, with a shiny peak, completed the outfit.

AGAIN THE car reached the southern entrance of the park and stopped. Ram Singh left the tonneau and resumed his seat beside the chauffeur, his job completed. The car turned east to Fifth Avenue and ran south.

"Are we going to a fancy dress ball?" asked Nita, looking at her companion in utter amazement and remembering what she, herself, looked like.

"We are going to pay a visit to Sylvester Bannister," Wentworth informed her, "at whose house our friend Commissioner Kirkpatrick has been invited—to his death!"

"But Sylvester Bannister lives somewhere in the sixties," she said, "and we are going south."

"Wait and see," he replied. "There are more surprises in store for you."

Southward the big car rolled smoothly and swiftly until they came to Washington Square, where it stopped at the northwest corner.

"This is where we get out," Wentworth said, and they alighted upon the sidewalk.

Immediately, and again without any direction from Wentworth, the car moved away and was gone. They were alone at Washington Square. Wentworth guided his companion half a block south and halted a decrepit taxicab.

"This is where we get in," he informed her, opening the door for her to enter the rickety affair.

Puzzled and excited by the adventure upon which she found herself, Nita entered the taxi. A man got off the driver's seat and walked away without saying a word. Wentworth took his place and started the taxi, turning north.

"Now that Molly and Jerry Stone are together again," remarked Wentworth to Nita through the open window, "I have two things yet to do. I must prevent good old Stanley Kirkpatrick from getting murdered tonight; and I must take Grogan's confession to the murder away from Mortimer Mack, so that I can give the Governor the necessary proof of the innocence of Molly's father."

"And what am I to do?" asked Nita.

"Perhaps nothing," he answered. "But wait and see." And he passed back to her, through the open window, a very tiny, but quite deadly, pistol.

NORTHWARD THE taxi rattled until they were in the sixties in the vicinity of Sylvester Bannister's big town house. On a corner, within view of the Bannister home, Wentworth stopped the taxi and they waited, watching the house.

The first person to arrive was Mortimer Mack, his little figure being easily recognized as he went up the steps.

"The first actor has arrived," commented Wentworth to Nita who was sitting tensely behind him in the cab, "unless, of course, there are others already in the house."

There was a wait of fifteen minutes before another car arrived before the Bannister house. From it three men alighted and trudged up the steps to the front door. At their head, limping very badly, Wentworth recognized the hulking form of Dan Grogan.

"It looks rather bad," he said to Nita. "There go the assassins—three of them! Are you still game to go through with it?"

"Try me," was all she said.

But Wentworth himself received a surprise, when, half an hour later, another car arrived and discharged a single passenger. It was Roberts, the President of the Board of Aldermen, one of the strongest and most incorruptible of the city officials.

Perhaps Roberts, the President of the Board of Alderman, and Stanley Kirkpatrick, the Commissioner of Police, were the two greatest obstacles to Mortimer Mack in his attempt to gain control of the politicians and so rule New York. These two men cared not a snap of their fingers for politicians, and death was the only means by which they could be overcome.

Then came Commissioner Kirkpatrick. He had no police escort with him, something he seldom used, and his car drove away and left him as his military figure ascended the steps to the front door.

"One of the cleverest men in New York, but for once he is blind," commented Wentworth to Nita. "I hope that I shall be able to save him."

Nor did Wentworth wait long before going into action, one of those desperate actions in which life and death hung in the balance, depending upon the quickness of his wit, the keenness of his eye and the steadiness of his aim.

"Do you see that hydrant in front of Bannister's house?" he asked Nita. "Walk over there and stand behind it. When I hit the hydrant, scream as loudly as you can and fall to the sidewalk as if dead. Whatever happens, pretend to be quite unconscious until I tell you to wake up. Understand?"

"Uh-huh," she replied a little breathlessly. "But for heaven's sake, don't let me get arrested in this costume!"

IN HIS big library Sylvester Bannister faced his guests, the Commissioner of Police and the President of the Board of Aldermen, across the shining top of his library table, upon which lay a single sheet of white paper.

Several times Kirkpatrick's alert eyes dropped from Bannister's face to that sheet of paper upon the table, which did not lie flat. It concealed something which would have been invisible to the Commissioner, had it not been partly reflected by the shining surface of the table.

Sylvester Bannister came straight to the point. Would Kirkpatrick and Roberts resign their official positions to accept high newspaper positions at double their present salaries?

Mortimer Mack, sitting meekly to one side, commenced to speak.

"Shut up!" ordered old Bannister in a commanding tone. "I'll do the talking."

Mortimer Mack closed his lips quickly. He was in the presence of his master. The quiet, elderly publisher had cowed him with a look and a few words.

"Well, what is your answer, gentlemen?" Bannister asked, looking directly at Commissioner Kirkpatrick. "Do you accept my very liberal offer?"

Commissioner Stanley Kirkpatrick's eyes glanced again at the big sheet of paper upon the table. Upon his face was some amusement and some contempt. Quickly his hand swept the sheet of paper from the table. From beneath it a small revolver fell from the table into a waste basket.

"So you are the master mind behind all this tampering with the politicians by Mortimer Mack, eh?" he questioned witheringly. "I suppose you wanted political power, eh? You were willing to seduce a lot of men through Mack, who made money out of it, and turn them into drug addicts. To get your ends you wrecked homes by using unscrupulous and licentious women, and you ruined other families through gambling. Now you try to bribe me, and—if I refuse—you are prepared to kill me. Well, Mr. Bannister, let me tell you that you are not clever enough to catch an old fox like me."

"You have evil thoughts, Mr. Commissioner," said old Bannister. "But since they are evil, let it be as you think."

He raised his hand slightly, and from behind the heavy drapes at the entrance there stepped forth Dan Grogan and his two companions. Each of the three men held an automatic pistol in his hand.

"Well, get it over with," directed Bannister coldly. "What are you waiting for?"

The three men slowly began to raise their pistols, while Mortimer Mack turned his head so that he would not see what was about to happen. Roberts, the President of the Board of Alderman, trembled and was too alarmed to move otherwise. Stanley Kirkpatrick faced the three murderers and deliberately laughed.

Suddenly, from the street, a terrific crash sounded, followed by a feminine scream.

The three men lowered their pistols somewhat. Grogan limped to a window, pulled the curtain aside and looked out.

"There has been an accident," he said, "and they are carrying somebody into the house."

"Get back behind the portières!" snapped Sylvester Bannister. "But be ready to kill these two men, if they make the slightest attempt to escape. Shoot them no matter what happens, or who is in the room, if they attempt to get away or even move from their chairs."

Quickly Grogan and his two companions slipped back behind the curtains.

Voices sounded in the hall and through the drapes staggered a tall taxi driver, with an apparently unconscious girl in his arms. The driver looked unusually tall because of a dirty, yellow coat buttoned tightly around his throat and reaching almost to his feet. As for the girl, she was cheaply and flashily dressed and her face was painted almost beyond belief. Over the man's arm her head hung downward with lifeless immobility.

Richard Wentworth and Nita had arrived.

FOR A moment Wentworth stared stupidly around the room. He knew, by the look of Roberts face, that a desperate situation existed, but he could not yet locate the danger. The grease smudge gave him so ridiculous an appearance that he appeared to be a man of small intellect and very much bewildered. Suddenly he darted forward and placed the inert girl in a chair near Bannister, while the servant, who had followed them in, brought a pillow and then withdrew at a nod from his master.

"Shall I call a police doctor for the young—ah—the young lady?" asked Kirkpatrick, audaciously reaching for the telephone.

"No!" barked Bannister savagely. "Probably she has just fainted."

Kirkpatrick's hand drew back from the telephone, while he watched Bannister pour some brandy into a glass from a decanter, evidently with the intention of trying to revive the girl.

"Are you the boss?"

Wentworth, in his capacity of a mentally upset taxi driver, stared wildly at Bannister as he asked the question. Abruptly, without waiting for an answer, his excitement increased and he began to walk crazily about the room. He shouted that it was not his fault that the girl had jumped in front of his taxi.

It was a beautiful piece of acting for the purpose of giving him time to find out what was wrong and where the danger lay. He flung his long arms about and stared around in an unbalanced manner. His excitement increased, and he began to run here and there about the room with his eyes upon the floor.

It was while Bannister was administering the brandy to the supposedly unconscious girl that the taxi man, during a sudden rush, kicked the waste basket almost the full length of the room. Wentworth had seen the revolver which lay in the waste basket—and he had also seen something else.

Out of the basket slid Bannister's revolver and came to rest within a foot of the curtains—just where the toe of a shoe showed beneath the drapery.

Wentworth seemed to see the revolver for the first time and halted above it as if transfixed. He seemed scared and absurdly puzzled at sight of the weapon. Slowly he bent down and reached for it, but drew his hand back like a child in fear. Again he reached for it and gingerly raised the revolver a few inches from the floor.

"Drop that!" called Bannister sharply, looking over his shoulder.

Wentworth started violently at the sudden command. It

seemed as though the sudden start caused him to press the trigger. There was a loud report from the revolver in his hand—and the man behind the drapery fell forward, clutched at his heart and lay still upon the floor.

From the opposite side of the entrance Grogan sprang forward, gun in hand. But Wentworth had dropped the small revolver and had jerked two heavy pistols from the pockets of his long, yellow coat. Faced by the tan man with two guns, Grogan let his own weapon crash upon the floor.

Banister dropped the liqueur glass and grabbed a pistol from the drawer of his table with unexpected quickness for such an elderly man.

"Don't try it!" said a cool, feminine voice from behind his back.

Nita had disobeyed her orders and had recovered consciousness before she had been told to do so. She was sitting up very straight and very much awake. In her hand was the small pistol, which she pressed into Bannister's back.

IT WAS then that the third hidden assassin stepped out from behind the drapes directly behind Wentworth.

"I've got 'em, boss," this man exclaimed. "I'll take the Commissioner of Police first."

There was no time for Wentworth to turn and fire. There was only one thing that he could do, and he did it…. He sprang sideways in front of his old friend Stanley Kirkpatrick!

From behind him came the crash of the thug's pistol and the bullet, intended for the Commissioner, tore into Wentworth's right shoulder.

The impact of the heavy slug caught him off balance and threw him to the floor. But even as he struck, he fired upward with his left hand and sent a bullet straight into the forehead of the man who had wounded him.

Grogan seized the opportunity to pick up the weapon he had dropped, and Mortimer Mack, in desperation, drew a small revolver from his pocket. Wentworth kicked the chair from under the little man, sending him to the floor, while he shot Grogan through the heart, just as the restaurant man fired, placing another bullet in Wentworth's right arm.

Wounded, bleeding and in pain, Wentworth rolled over upon the floor toward Mortimer Mack, and succeeded somehow in knocking the weapon from the little man's hand before that badly startled man could regain his feet. In another moment he had jerked Mack's pocketbook out and was shaking the contents out upon the floor with his one useful hand. Abruptly he snatched one of the fallen papers.

"Here you are, Commissioner," he said, holding the paper up to the surprised but self-controlled Kirkpatrick.

"Here is Grogan's confession to the murder of Mack's partner. I had Bannister's telephone wire tapped and I heard him order little Mortimer Mack to bring it down to him tonight. This will clear the man, Dennis, who is waiting electrocution at Sing Sing. Just attend to the matter for me, will you Commissioner?"

Then, for the first time, Commissioner Kirkpatrick lost some of his self-control and became just a trifle emotional.

"Dick," he asked, in a voice that trembled slightly, "is it really you? Dick, old man, you offered your life when you saved mine by jumping in front of that thug's gun. Dick, will you ever forgive me for suspecting you of anything wrong?"

"Oh, shut up!" exclaimed Wentworth, sitting up a little gingerly. "Meet Nita! She is right behind you."

"Nita!" exclaimed Kirkpatrick in more amazement as he turned around to look at her. "By the great horned spoon, that's the cleverest make-up I ever saw!"

But Nita had really fainted at sight of Wentworth's wounds and sat—unconscious—with her little pistol still pressed into the back of Sylvester Bannister!

POPULAR PUBLICATIONS
HERO PULPS

LOOK FOR MORE SOON!

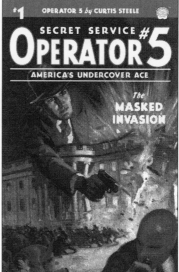